The Safe House

Tom Fisher

Published by **Crusader eBooks**, Perth, Western Australia

Copyright Tom Fisher 2012

Cover Design by Tom Fisher

Typeset by the author in Times New Roman.

National Library of Australia Cataloguing-in-Publication entry:

Author: Fisher, Tom.

Title: Outbound / Tom Fisher.

ISBN-10: 0-9872987-3-9, ISBN-13: 978-0-9872987-3-7

Dewey Number: A823.4

Chapters:

Chapter One

The crowded conference room was sweltering, the air close and hot even with the windows open and overhead fans spinning. Why on earth they had to hold these things in high summer when even travel was a chore, Sam Flanagan thought to himself. Parliamentary recess, they'd said.

No filming or cameras were allowed, tough call for a film-maker at such an historic event, so he sat back against the side wall watching the proceedings, pricking his ears up only when his old friend Bertram stood to speak, asserting his right as an elder to be there and his right to speak, before sitting down again to draw his impassive mask of a face back into himself.

The rest of the tribal elders went through the same process one after another, until finally a wasted scarecrow of an old man emanating awesome power stood to register his presence.

Sam watched him curiously. He reminded him of Vincent; not only in character but in the way others quietly deferred to him, and made way for him. There was an elderly white man in his group with another younger man who looked like he might be his son, and next to him a second thin blackfellow with the same dark piercing gaze as the old man at the podium.

"Who are that mob, Peter?" he leaned aside to whisper.

"That old fella, Everard Foley; Queensland side mob, Talaria Station mob, Eurongera side, you know. That other whitefella, that one there, 'is name Ned Collins. Big station owner, but went bush long time, like us mob now, that fella. That next fella 'is son, Angus Collins. That other fella, Edwin Foley, Everard grandson. They all the same brother-mob, you know, that mob; proper businessmen, been through all the ceremonies, everything, like old time; proper big fellas, right across."

Sam's young protégé Alex sitting nearby listened carefully, watching patiently until the room went quiet and he felt eyes on him suddenly. The boy looked up to see the old crone of a man at the podium had finished speaking, but remained there gazing solemnly at him, then at his tribal brother Peter in the seat next to his, until the other younger fellow Edwin glanced up and murmured something, and he stood down.

Everard was the last of the old Traditional Law men to introduce themselves, and with that business out of the way they'd be breaking up for lunch.

Sam and Bertram sat back with Alex and Peter waiting for the room to clear. As the four of them stood finally one of the small boys from the Western Queensland group picked his way carefully across the big room and asked if they'd like to join them for lunch. Acknowledging the mob across the room standing patiently waiting for them, they went out their own door and slowly walked through the corridors following the posters to the big dining room, where they were met by two more boys and escorted to their table.

Sam took his turn to watch and listen carefully as introductions were made. The old white man sitting there was indeed the reclusive Ned Collins, son-in-law of legendary old-time cattleman Don McKenzie of Eurongera they said, who'd be a legend in his own right were he not so quiet in his manner. His eldest son there with him was Angus, who cattlemen feared to their marrow for his uncanny ability to know what was going to happen just before they did, and his second son Hamish who was himself a strange, distant fellow. Next to be introduced were grandsons Alexander - who he introduced to Alex as Young Sandy, of Talaria Station - and young Arthur who smiled a lot and everyone called Artie Boy, then finally granddaughter Ellie MacFarlane with three boys of her own, who'd been acting as messengers.

The old men sat when chairs were pulled out for them, not saying much, then once they were comfortable the rest of the party took their seats. Before they settled old Everard spoke softly and a murmur ran down the table for Alex and Peter to go up to the head and sit with him, so there was a fair bit of jostling suddenly as people changed places.

While lunch was served and plates passed back and forth Everard sat closely observing the proceedings. Alex could feel the traditional elder's piercing gaze, just as the old man Vincent had done with him in the sacred cave at Puntayeri not so many years before, and he responded the same way, looking in askance.

"That one your brother, properly," Everard said finally, indicating Peter. He reached over and placing his gnarled hand on Ned's shoulder added, "This one my brother, all the same."

He turned to Angus then, and Edwin. "This two fella, same like us; proper brother, from old time business. That one Angus belong this brother Ned. This one Edwin belong my old brother; same father, same mother with me. Pinish up that one; gone now, all right? Call this one nephew, like that."

Alex nodded. They were watching him, reading him, all of them; the two white men quite as intently as the others.

"We've heard a lot about you, young Lennox," Angus broke the ice finally in his oddly clipped late Victorian accent. "Jolly good to meet you at last, good to see you've come up for the show."

Alex nodded again shyly, but Angus pressed him, "What do you reckon about all this?"

"Not much," he replied after a moment. "The same old bullshit, except I heard there was going to be a bit of a summit behind the scenes, with all you blokes after the politicians have gone." He frowned slightly. "That's why I came."

"Worried about it, are you?"

"No, not really, except I hear you fellas have freehold title over there in Queensland, from the old McKenzie era. Somebody said you've got a lot of country down south too, that some of your people have moved back to. These Warmunya and Puntayeri fellas here are on crown land."

Sam watched as they spoke, wishing again that he'd had his camera on them.

The old white bloke Ned nodded to himself before taking a big mouthful of prime steak and chewing it awhile glanced back up, flicking the thick wad of fillet into his cheek like a plug of tobacco before speaking.

He leaned forward, pointing with his table knife, staring, emphatic, "Wasn't always like that, son. After I left school we had to bring them all up north, you know, away from the Welfare. Just before the war it was, 1937, at the start of that big war drought that lasted seven years, Biblical, all the big inland rivers dried up, a plague on the land. All those old families came with us, all the way north with us by camel wagon, Abdul Achmed driving and my uncle Don McKenzie boss while my old schoolmate Ian Ramsay bless his soul kept the books, with the rest of us stringing two and a half thousand head of cattle, did you know that? Ellie's grandfather-in-law Andrew MacFarlane overseer. I'll tell you about it sometime."

He stopped to finish his mouthful, swallowing finally. "To answer your question, son, that sacred country you mention is not ours either, along the lakes there. We never got to take it up like we wanted."

"Really? Is that right?" Alex paused, frowning. "Um, can I ask you something else then, about yourself? What school did you go to? You have an accent."

"Mount Tambla. We have an Angus stud down that way that we set up for them, just before the Second War when the CSIRO was being set up, about when the drought took hold. Used to call it the Advisory Committee on Science and Industry, did you know that?"

Alex leaned forward, taking a liking to the old man. "Yes, I think we'll get along real good, what do you reckon?"

"Could be, son," Ned replied. "Can you ride a horse? Come back over to Eurongera when we leave, if you like, after these big-wig political cunts go back to Canberra or wherever hell place they belong. I'll show you around."

"Really?" Alex beamed, glancing back down the table at Sam seeking his approval.

"Yes, all right, it'll be all right," he replied. "Sam doesn't have to be back for another month or two, and we don't have to be back ourselves for six weeks yet."

Everard and Edwin both watched him, eyes smiling in impassive black faces, while Sam looked away, thinking his own thoughts.

Chapter Two

On the long slow drive home, with the big regional meeting out of the way finally, the mixed party headed south then easterly through Oodnadatta, skirting the Simpson Desert away to their north until passing through north of Lake Eyre they were into more-or-less wooded country, then east along the northern reaches of the Srzelecki Desert. Across the Queensland border finally they carefully traversed the myriad dry streamlets of the Overflow country that drained south when it rained, then turned southeast again toward Eurongera proper.

Sam had decided not to come, but return instead to Adelaide to write up his report on the meeting before relocating to Western Australia for a film contract. Bertram simply flew back north to Warmunya with his own people. Eurongera Pastoral Company would fly the two lads back to Adelaide if need be in time for their new semester.

Day after long day under the great open sky marked only by wispy white cloud formations high above, as they carefully negotiated the rough bush tracks Alex and Peter alternated their time between talking with the children and old people, and listening in on the daily radio schedule keeping everyone in touch with the outside world. They stopped and camped, and ate and slept, and woke again to relieve themselves; avoiding for no particular reason the politics and argument occupying Angus and the other men, yet marveling at their organization and cool proficiency.

The country was parched this time of year, the heat haze shimmering and the going tough so they stopped to rest during the day, making their steady way across dry country in the cool of evening and early morning.

On the last leg of the journey, up along the western shore of the most northerly lake they encountered along the way, the convoy stopped to rest. This end of the lake was rimmed with steep banks. While the water level was low it had been a good winter with late rain, and there were literally thousands of birds on the glistening water and in the trees, flocking close to the oasis amid the hundreds of miles of semi-desert the convoy had traversed.

Further out the lake petered off into shallows, and finally into vast shimmering salt clay pans that would fill to overflow sometime when it rained again, maybe in the next generation if the climate held. Here in close under the steep banks and ungrazed native trees, however, it was cool and shady.

Alex opened the door of the Landcruiser and swung his legs down, but didn't get out yet and sat there taking in the view, heels on the door sill. Eventually he noticed Angus gazing across at him.

"It's lovely," he said back across finally. "We have a little place over in the Territory, did you know, that we pegged out. It's very nice like this. You can't see it from up on the plain, looking across; you have to find it. We take gold from a seam along the side of the gully, above the water, if we need a bit of loose change sometimes."

Angus simply nodded. His tribal twin brother-friend - his parallel self Edwin - indicated the rough direction with his lips, watching his face.

"That how we know you, Alecki," Edwin said softly; "all our mob here. That dreaming place from old time, same like this place. We show you, same story, all right?"

Alex stared at them, and then shrugged and said out loud, challenging. "Nothing surprises me anymore, about you fellas. But it's not connected to Puntayeri, is it? That's bullshit, except they own part shares now, in the Anamenatjere mine. Their story runs up into the Sandy Desert to the north-west, and southwest again all the way through Western Australia. Over this side the stories run north and south more, don't they, once you get through the Centre? It's your place, isn't it."

Nobody said anything, just watched him, so he sat still until finally he gazed about once more, watching the great flocks screeching and circling among the trees, bickering over perching space along the branches. The sky was entirely cloudless and the flocks of birds set off the clear blue - the brilliant white cockatoos, great brown and white pelicans, black shags, grey herons, pink and grey galahs, the soft grey-browns of crested pigeons with bright flashes of ruby and emerald on their wings that the boys skillfully snared for the pot, and not least the mottled rainbow greens of uncountable millions of tiny budgerigars whirring past in their endlessly confused disorder. He was moved suddenly, and glanced across.

"Have you ever seen anything so beautiful?" he said. "I'd live out here forever, you know."

"Not our place, Alex. This is all National Parks now, you know that."

He turned to find old Ned standing nearby, also watching him. Everard approached from behind him again and beckoned to him, then to Peter in turn, so the two boys got down and as the old men turned to walk away they followed them.

As they walked Angus and Edwin fell in behind them, causing the women to glance over from where they'd begun to settle there in the shade of the trees along the edge of the water, and murmur among themselves.

Ned half-turned to them as they went. "Show you around, eh?" he said quietly before walking on ahead, following Everard. Alex felt hazy suddenly, as if his vision blurred, and he blinked. He stopped and shook his head; thinking to clear away whatever it was that entered his thoughts, but Peter next to him simply smiled.

"What are you doing?" Alex wanted to know.

"Comin' up story time, eh? Like that old fella pinish up, Puntayeri side, tell 'im story you."

Alex stopped. He stood away slightly, out of the group. He gazed back at them, one to the other before turning to his friend.

"Peter, do you mean that time I was hypnotised, when I couldn't remember who I was, when I first got there?"

"Little bit like that, eh?"

"Why?"

Peter hesitated a moment. The others watched his face as he glanced away, and then looked back at Alex.

"You still like white fella little bit too much," Peter explained. "Know something, like us, but can't remember. White fella lost, you know, can't think properly. You're good fella, good brother to me. We teach you properly now."

"Is that why I'm here?"

"Only partly," Ned broke in. "You're good, everybody likes you. Old fella like me, well, I grew up in the bush. But I didn't hear the singing myself until later, nearly too late, you know, but that's past isn't it. Right now, we've all been watching you, son, a few years now. You're lucky we got onto you when we did."

"Why lucky, Mr Collins?" he replied, abrupt. "I work hard. What makes me lucky?"

They all looked at him, then Everard turned on his heel and walked back to where the vehicles were parked.

The women by this time had begun to set up camp and some of the children were in the water swimming and splashing about. Alex strode down to the edge of the water and leaving his clothing piled neatly on a fallen tree promptly jumped in after them. Peter followed close behind while the other men went off to unload the vehicles and help the women.

When they finished Ned broke off and piling his own clothes next to the boys' there on the log waded into the water. Alex watched him intently; for an old man he possessed a good physique still, unabashed and at home in the water. In his prime he must have weighed over 100 kilos, all solid muscle without an ounce of fat but big in the shoulders and torso after a lifetime in the stock saddle. He glanced up the bank at his son Angus who was much slimmer; lithe, sensual in the way he moved his body like a trained cavalry rider, or dancer perhaps, except for the odd way he held his head as if he had a permanent crick in his neck.

His mind wandered a little, thinking what a fine figure that Angus would pose on a good stock horse, his posture denoting more arrogance than injury, lending itself to dressage were it not for his way with cattle, but at that moment Ned came alongside and touching his shoulder bade him follow.

He looked back at Peter who'd already turned to play with the younger boys, then toward Ned who waded toward a projecting sandbank where he sat on a log sticking out into the shallows. He came up and sat next to him, and glanced up, listening.

"What made you knock 'em back just now, son, those old fellas?" Ned wanted to know.

He sucked in his breath, then shrugged and let it out.

"Ah, well, I've been fair through a lot of stuff with them - with Peter, you know - and it's not my cup of tea, really. It's like the tykes, and these guys are like priests - once they've got their hooks into your soul they won't let go - and I wasn't raised like that. I'll meet my own Maker when I'm good and ready, that's my own opinion, and make my peace with Him then."

He turned to the old man on the log next to him, feet dangling in the cool water. "I don't want to talk about it, if it's OK with you."

"No worries, young fella, just curious. Our McKenzie mob were all proud, canny old Scottish Presbyterians, so I know all about it. I think we've all got along together so well because we each have our integrity and our own way about us, only crossing over and back when it suits us, and when there's good reason."

"All right, I thought that, but like I said I don't want to talk about it." Alex paused. "Tell me instead where we are, precisely. Where is this place? What's going on?"

"Back across that way," Ned began, "right over the other side of these lakes, where you come up on the long stock route through western New South Wales; about thirty mile from here, that's where these cunts hooked me good and proper. I married my cousin Elizabeth soon after that, up on Eurongera Station which is over that way," he pointed easterly. "When we went south again we had Angus, and Hamish not long after."

"That old fella Vincent from Warmunya, that old boss of Puntayeri, you know," he went on, "he was a proper old Law Man, the last of them. I know, and you know; you have his fat on you. But well before our time that other old fella, from this place here, who was proper tribal brother to the previous owner of all this, my mother's great uncle Sandy McKenzie; same name as you, Alexander. That old fella was deadly serious, proper magic man. He was Everard's grandfather, same name as your brother now, that Peter, you know."

Ned glanced at Alex who was listening intently, eyes distant.

"I'm telling you now, son, for your own sake, and I lie to no man, that old man Peter Foley is the one who kept my cousin Angus McKenzie here after he was killed in a riding accident."

Alex turned to gaze at him, but thoughtfully.

"That's your son Angus, that's him, isn't it?" he asked after a moment.

Ned looked away, and then tossed his head slightly. "What do you make of that?" he wanted to know suddenly.

"They say out here there are children dreaming places," Alex replied thoughtfully after a moment. "I don't really understand things like that, but it doesn't matter, does it? We don't die anyway; we just come and go, forever. It's all, like, country, isn't it? It wouldn't really be too hard for an old-time magic man to steal a newly dead child's ghost and tuck it away somewhere, and wait for a chance for him to be born again, back into this world. Because, maybe, there was a reason he shouldn't have died, but something happened that shouldn't have happened?"

The old man nodded, glancing affectionately at him.

"But coming back to the present, this present business," Alex continued carefully, "is I made a mistake setting up that Anamenatjere consortium without consulting you fellas."

He sat back, breathing easily now, nodding to himself, glad to be free.

He leaned forward again.

"Mr Collins," he went on, "please offer my apology. I'm young and get carried away, but my intentions are good. We only wanted to let the Warmunya Community have some money, without the Welfare getting too nosey. There's not that much, only cash if somebody needs something or some job needs to be done. I don't know how we can share it, financially anyway. I don't think it can be resolved that way. I don't think I should be taken to task for it either, by you or by them. Better if we maybe fly your mob up to Warmunya some time for a reckoning - they suffer the insult after all. But we didn't mean it like that. Those people have nothing, while your mob at least have their cattle. Bertram is a very wise man; he is the inheritor from Vincent. Your people here are also wise, and acting in a good way, but I'm really just a sort of precocious kid who's lucky most things turn out all right, more or less, but shit, I can't be held responsible in the same way they can."

He slid off the log and waded into the water a way, bending over to splash water on himself, as if to rinse the thing clean.

He stood and turned, naked in the water and a glint in his eye but with the sun behind him making the ripples sparkle, as if he were part of it.

"OK," he said finally. "Formally, I do need to ask you to help me with this. I can't ask them because they're one side, and I can't ask the others because they're the other side, and I have no standing because I just a kid, but that's the reason you're here talking to me, isn't it. You can see the dilemma. It's their business."

Ned inclined his head thoughtfully, then glanced up.

"What do you want me to do, son?"

Alex jerked his head up, and paused, then walked up onto the sandy bank to the fallen tree to gather up his clothes.

"Don't bullshit, Mr Collins. You know that," he said on the way past.

The old fellow stared, then chuckled, then picking up his own clothes stood to follow.

Chapter Three

There was food ready for them when they came back up from their swim. The others had eaten so Alex and Ned sat quietly finishing off the last scraps before clearing the dishes, and washing them packed everything neatly into the truck. Peter was in a huddle with Everard and Edwin, talking softly, while Angus had gone off for a walk with the smaller boys, showing them around.

The radio crackled and Ned went to answer it, speaking only briefly before turning back to Alex.

"It's Sam," he said. "You're not flying back to Adelaide. He wants you in Perth when you're done here with us."

Alex looked intently at him before glancing away.

"Did you ask him if Peter got in too?" he said, looking back.

"Just passing on the message, son. He said he wants you both. Don't worry about your gear, he'll get it packed and sorted. What's up?"

"Well, he was offered some sort of adjunct position at the University of Perth, over in Western Australia, in Celtic and Indigenous Law, before we came up to Alice for the big meeting. Before he took the job he wanted to see if we'd be offered places there too instead of Adelaide, you know, as undergraduates."

He glanced back at Ned, thoughtfully, before gazing across to Peter sitting there with the old Law Men. He was already looking at him.

Peter silently flicked his hand in sign language. What's happening?

"Looks like we're going to Perth," Alex said, loudly enough for everyone to hear. "We're not going back to Adelaide. When we're finished here we'll fly straight across, maybe."

He stopped suddenly as a thought came to his mind.

"Or maybe we'll go to Melbourne first and stay with Edie for a couple of days, I think," he added suddenly, "and fly over from there."

Peter nodded, flicking a glance quickly at Ned before returning to his conversation with Edwin.

"You'd better tell him to register our acceptances," Alex went on, "or if he can't do it without our signatures fax the forms to Auntie Edie and we'll sort it when we get to Melbourne."

"He can fax them to Eurongera if you like; they'll be there at the homestead by time we arrive, and we can fax them straight back to Perth for you. We won't be in Melbourne for weeks yet, and those acceptances have to be in quick, before the next round of offers goes out."

"All right, do that. That'll be good. Thanks, Mr Collins."

Angus returned with the children, gazing intently at Alex as they came into camp. A quick look from Ned and they turned away.

"My Auntie Ellie made me matriculate, you know, Alex," Ned said to him, "but after she died and I got the corporate structure in place to manage the whole shebang I went bush. I raised my family out here basically; back and forth. We traverse half the bloody continent, when it's all said and done."

He sat carefully watching the boy's face. "Our company headquarters are stationed down there on Wyandera, still, and our research station at Belkoomie on the Murray has turned out some really very good, practical veterinary scientists over the years, aside from our first class Angus bulls and heifers, did you know that?"

The old man sighed and turned away, gazing off toward the horizon while Alex waited for him to finish.

When he said nothing more Alex stepped toward him and said, "We all have to do things both ways now, Mr Collins, if you don't mind me saying, like you have. It's not the one way or the other anymore; we all have to go both ways. Our mob at Warmunya are learning from the old

Territory side mob as well, up in Arnhem Land, and they're very happy for us to come down here with you, but you're a lot more isolated here where you are. Funny, isn't it; you're closer in but in many ways you're a lot more remote than we're ever going to be."

Ned glanced at him, and nodded quietly to himself.

"All right," he said finally. "We'll get this Anamenatjere business out of the way; that's your place up there, where your gold mine is, and then we can have a bit of a yarn."

He turned away, looking across to Angus waiting patiently there with the children, but then glanced back at Alex.

"Might fly down to Melbourne with you, eh? Lady Bauer, your Auntie Edie, is a major shareholder of ours, still after all these years; when we first floated the company she came straight on board. She's been my contact with civilisation all this time, I bet you didn't know that either."

He paused a moment, nodding to himself, gazing thoughtfully across the lake. "You're right, young fella, we'll see about getting undergraduate scholarships organised for these remote area kids as well. We've have a bursary down at Mount Tambla since before the war, so this'll be right up our alley."

He nodded as he turned back to his family. "You're right, son," he repeated, "I knew there was a reason we should run into one another."

Alex watched as the old man started walking away, then called to him.

"Mr Collins, tell me, what do you call this country?" he called him back. "Not what they call it, those blackfellas; what do you call it? What did your legendary Uncle Don McKenzie of Eurongera call it? Your father-in-law, and what else?"

Ned stopped, and turned slowly, eyeing him. After a moment he said, "Don't go there, if you want to stay friends with me. Get your facts right, Don McKenzie was my mother's first cousin. He was old Don McKenzie's son, Sandie's older brother Don. That Don; that we'd be talking about, was young Don. He was my first cousin once removed."

Alex's eyes narrowed. "If you don't mind my saying so, you're not telling the whole truth. I mean no disrespect, sir, but I need you to trust me. I really only asked you what did he call this country, not about your family. You don't need to be suspicious."

He stood back a moment before turning to look the old man in the eye. He took a breath.

"If I wanted to probe I'd be asking how old Sandie McKenzie's son Angus happens to be the same man as your own son Angus, except he was a boy, back then. But I didn't ask you before, you asked me. I showed you respect, and didn't go really into it, about how he was killed in the first place."

He stood his ground.

The old man nodded, cocking his head thoughtfully. He came back toward him and taking his arm turned to point north and northwest.

"Way up there, son, right across" he said quietly, "is what we call the Overflow. All that rain falling in the event, when it we get it, runs back south-westerly where it runs into Lake Eyre, over there," he turned about, pointing with his lips after the Aboriginal fashion.

He turned further, westerly, following around, taking the boy with him by the arm.

"West of where we are now is the Strzelecki Desert, then you hit Lake Frome on the South Australian side before you get into the Flinders Ranges."

Skipping the vast expanse of red gibber desert horizon to the west they continued turning to face south.

"Down that way, this lake system runs into that big breakaway you can just make out on the horizon. Can you see? That long shadow there, where the clouds hang about twenty mile south of the first lake down there. Those clouds aren't off the lake; they come up over the breakaway.

It marks the southern boundary of this, sort of, bioregion as they call it these days. South of there is a bit of a drive through open gibber country, before you get back into the long paddocks that take you way south into the Riverina. Takes about six weeks to drive a big mob all the way, then another three weeks into South Australia, if that's where you're headed, or a week into the western slopes where the really good grazing is."

He looked down at him, not unfondly. "Depends where you're headed, doesn't it son, and what you want to do when you get there. And where you're coming from, eh?"

Chapter Four

"Do you think I upset them?" Alex wanted to know, quietly, as he gazed out the window of the airplane following the towering jagged cliffs of the coastline far below.

"No," Peter answered eventually, looking up from his Phantom comic, then gently, "you'll be right. Everybody like you. You bloody argue all the time, that's all, with everybody, but that your dreaming. You're like that little tjilpa, that hunting quoll, you know. That old fella Everard call you *Tjilpa*."

Alex glanced at him then away again. The weeks up on Eurongera Station riding around the cattle, getting to know Ellie's three boys who'd seriously taken to him and shown him a trick or two when it came to bushcraft, swimming in the lovely homestead billabong during the heat of the day, and the sublime mid-summer evenings on the big front verandah with the cattlemen and a cold beer, had given him a whole new lease on life after five intense years with Peter studying for his tertiary entry.

While he spent nearly all his time with Ned, learning about the cattle business and paying special attention to what he was saying about land titles, he'd been attracted to the middle boy, the one they called Little Artie as distinct from his Uncle Artie Boy. Little Artie sought him out at every opportunity and stuck with him like glue every time they went swimming, and crept into his room every night to sleep on an open swag next to his bed.

Those three boys were very good-looking, part-Aboriginal going back a bit. The older boy Donnie was taciturn and kept to himself like his legendary namesake, while the youngest boy Neddie was a dreamer like his great-grandfather. It was maybe because he and Little Artie were both second sons, Alex had first thought, until he realised that the boy threw back to his great-grandfather, Andrew MacFarlane, who'd been Don McKenzie's stock overseer and married one of the part-Aboriginal girls off Dadjari Station. And then again, children growing up on the remote cattle stations missed out on a lot of social interaction, not like the big crowded city schools, and had a way of attaching themselves to people. Most Aboriginal kids were the same.

Anyway, he liked the pretty girls at college, and the way he could charm them right into his arms with his sophisticated good looks and ready wit. Having a ten year-old boy manoeuvre his way so subtly and skillfully into his sense of himself like that gave him pause. When they left for Melbourne Little Artie was nowhere to be seen.

Peter glanced at him suddenly, reading his mind.

"That Little Artie like you, everybody can see. You his proper hero number one, but you don't look after him properly like big brother. What's goin' on?"

He waited awhile before answering, his mind deflected suddenly by their flight out over the sea, with the Great Australian Bight coastline to the north now, but then he sat back and shrugged.

"You remember that Walt Whitman? That American poet we studied?" he said instead. "The old Yanks were worth something in those days; him and Mark Twain, you know."

He sat forward in his seat, fist raised. *"Have you learned the lessons only of those who admired you, and were tender with you, and stood aside for you? Have you not learned great lessons from those who braced themselves against you, and disputed passage with you?"* he recited out loud.

Peter looked at him and patiently shook his head. "Yeah, well, shut up now, eh? Not like that anymore, bloody Yanks," he murmured, and went back to his comic.

Alex simply nodded and went back to looking out the window, lost in thought. After a while he leaned back the other way.

"There was this American judge," he said quietly, wanting to make his point. "A while ago he said in one of his legal determinations, '*Enforced silence on disturbing facts does not clear the air'*. My Dad told me that, you know, one night when he was really pissed, and pissed off about something, real big. I mean, he seriously glared at me about it, like it was my fault, or I had to fix it, or something. But it was a state parliament issue and he was trying to get it through the media without being sued, so I thought I'm just a kid why are you asking me. Fuck him anyway."

Peter glanced at him and shrugged, and he sighed to himself and looked down.

"What do you reckon about that Phantom, in that stupid comic you're reading, eh?" Alex persisted.

Peter glanced up sharply, then chuckled and leaned back in his seat.

"Purple fuckin' tights, eh?" he murmured. "Most white fella got suits and uniforms, and funny hats, but this fella got purple tights; fuckin' underpants outside, like that Superman fella, except he got stripes."

"What's funny about that?"

"This Phantom fella, 'e live in this fuckin' Skull Cave, eh? Got 'im big white 'orse, pet dingo, girlfriend, underground tunnel, tell 'im Governor what to do, save all this stupid black bastard from this other whitefella mob. Silly cunt, can't believe it, eh."

"Maybe just an arguer, do you reckon?" Alex replied after a moment. "Trouble with all you stupid black bastards, you don't know what parody is, no sense of bloody humour."

Peter went back to his comic.

Chapter Five

Alex was surprised when they landed in Perth finally to find it was still daylight, when his watch said 10:15 pm. There was a three-hour delay between Melbourne's eastern standard daylight saving time and Perth's west coast time. Sam stared at him a moment before saying quietly that he should have known better, except Peter butted in to say he'd been playing silly buggers all the way, and not paying attention.

At that Alex reached over and cuffed him.

Another thing they noticed as they made their way out to the car and drove into town from the airport was how dried-out and brown everything was. It wasn't the dry air and bright light, they were used to that from living out in the desert, but over here there was a winter wet-season that brought lush growth through spring that shriveled and died by Christmas, making the place look dead. Tree-trunks, buildings and footpaths were stained brown from the iron-laden groundwater used to water what was left of lawn around what looked like local council buildings. The rest of it looked like the same rundown American style post-war strip development found anywhere - old pubs, petrol stations, 1950s residential blocks.

Peter quickly buried himself back in his pile of phantom comics.

"Welcome to Perth," Sam said, "State of Excitement."

Eventually they made their way across a long bridge with a muddy scrub-covered sand island in the middle of the stream and turned through a roundabout into the city proper. There seemed to be a lot of old brick buildings being torn down and not-quite skyscrapers going up, with cranes dotting the skyline, but apart from that their impression of the place didn't change.

Alex thought a lot later, after all the trouble blew up, that the place had a sort of awkwardly cultivated, self-conscious, "big country town" image that it wanted to present to visitors, as if to hide something else, but it didn't quite work.

He wasn't fooled. He'd travelled around the bush with his Dad when he was little, back when they still got along. Victoria had big country towns, infused with an old-established civic pride, and so did New South Wales along the western slopes at any rate, with the grand old station homesteads further west, and this was not one of them. Here was sand and sand and sand, with the light so bright you had to shade your eyes, and dead grass and exhausted grey-green trees and red-brown stained buildings, and dry swamps littered with junk and salty air blowing in on a constant irritating sea breeze that at least cooled things down and relieved the heat tension if nothing else, though it made the day humid. They called it The Doctor.

There was something else he couldn't quite place; something about the people, who never really looked at each other. Only later, when he thought about it, he realised that it was their gushing hail-fellow-well-met manner of greeting one another that annoyed him, while those around them stared fixedly away. Peter simply fobbed them all off as *Gadiya*, which Alex thought was really childish, like his reading endless Phantom comics, until almost too late he understood that was what protected him psychologically in a world that made no sense to him anyway.

It was evening, and once through the city Sam pulled off the road into a big old vacant lot with a hamburger bar in a caravan parked in the middle with a sign that said 'Bernie's'. The service was friendly and down to earth, and their big burgers were fantastic.

The drive home along the river road toward the university took his breath away.

Alex relaxed a little after that, except that nothing seemed to fit, as if the burger bar had been beamed in from some Arizona desert and set there among the building rubble half under a bridge. The old brewery there on the river as they passed by was derelict while the weed-infested slopes to their right did nothing to enhance the view. The night lights strung along the river foreshore were strategic and deliberate.

Their flat when they arrived in Nedlands finally was small, like Sam's place in Adelaide five years ago when they first came down from the

Central Desert, before they moved into the big apartment overlooking the park. But they were twelve then, and now they were seventeen, tall and gangling in their late adolescence. At least Sam had the sense to set himself up, shifting the double bed into the smaller spare room leaving the big main bedroom with two single beds for Peter and Alex to share, although there was only a small shower recess with a toilet and wash basin so they'll have to take turns.

The place was musty, rank with generations of students, and the ancient enameled gas stove in the kitchenette let off a perpetual odour of moldy stale food and dead cockroaches no matter how much the thing was scrubbed. They didn't have to do much to settle in - no doubt about Sam, as a film-maker a master of logistics and breathtakingly precise in his methods - so the place was already well organised. He'd set his editing bench up in the living room with two smaller desks for the boys while they stepped gingerly around his cameras and gear. Good thing there was a breakfast bar with stools where they could take their meals.

By the time Alex adjusted his watch there was an extra three hours in the day. They were exhausted after being up early for a formal French breakfast with Auntie Edie in Toorak, then seeing old Ned Collins off on the train at Spencer Street, departing for Mount Tambla and his Belkoomie Research Station where he'd decided to call in and complete some business before heading back north.

As soon as they finished their delicious Bernie's burgers and some ice cream that Sam had in the fridge, the two boys took a cold shower and crashed under clean sheets.

Chapter Six

Still not having adjusted to the time delay they were up again early next morning. Sam was still asleep so they raided the fridge again and made themselves a huge breakfast of bacon and eggs, with hot toast and fresh coffee. The kitchen bustle and aroma from the percolator soon had Sam out of bed too.

It was a couple of hours away yet, but their first task this morning was to go across to the University and enroll. To take up time until the student office opened they unpacked their travel bags and went down to a Laundromat to get some washing done, and that out of the way sat with Sam to go over his film scripts and some of his early footage.

Their initial enthusiasm waned quickly, and they sat back frowning.

Alex turned to Sam. "This is crap," he said, "what's going on?"

Sam nodded quietly before asking, almost rhetorically, "What's wrong with it?"

"What? No good, boss, humbug, too much gammon," Peter butted in. "You know what's wrong. You can see."

"I want you to tell me."

"All right," Alex leaned forward. "Technically it's excellent, I mean, your camera work's just great, and the light is fantastic - one thing I'll say about this place, the clean air and the light quality - but where's your soul? This is not a Sam Flanagan film, it's somebody else's; they're just using you as a cameraman, and telling you where they want the thing pointed, at what they want, avoiding the reality. I mean, it's propaganda, crap; no narrative structure, no plot, no style, just legalistics and hypotheticals. You know what I mean."

Sam gazed fixedly at them, at one and the other and back again, apology all over his face.

"That's the brief. I'm sorry I didn't go over it properly to ensure enough field footage, or do any background checks before I took the job. I was more worried about you boys getting your places here, and anyway I was distracted by the Alice Springs trip."

The boys threw concerned glances at each other.

"What's it worth to you?"

"Well, it's a lot of money, too good to pass up."

"That's not what we wanted to know, Sam. I reckon, if it doesn't add anything to your folio, why not have your name removed from the credits and let them have what they want? And take the money."

Sam sighed. "Politics. They want my name. That's why they went to all the trouble to get me over here. That's the deal."

"Ha! Bullshit! We'll see about that. If it went to court we could easily demonstrate that this is atypical work. It's entirely different from any of your stuff, or anything on your academic record. Tell them to bugger off."

"There's no artistic freedom clause in the contract, Alex. The best thing I can do is argue with them about direction. I'm notionally the director, but I don't really have a choice because the brief is very specific, and it's their case data they want publicised. The best I can do with it is keeping me in the background and them taking the limelight."

He sat back shaking his head, frowning, dismissing further discussion. "Ah, leave it, OK? I'll see what I can do. I just wanted your opinion first."

Standing, he said abruptly, "All right, get dressed and we'll go across and get you enrolled. I'll show you around campus, eh?"

Leaving the camera and computers on they quickly changed into clean town clothes and followed Sam out the door and downstairs. The University was only a few blocks away so they walked. This part of the city was much nicer, with shady well-watered streets and a lot of new buildings completed. Aside from the contrast between the old established architecture with its residual Federation red brick and later Art Deco overtones, and the low-slung Mediterranean sandstone look consistent with campus policy, the surrounding streets were busy and focused.

As it turned out the office was open early, anticipating the influx of enrolling students, so rather than take Sam's guided tour they joined the queue and sent him off to do whatever he had to do.

It was boring, waiting and waiting and waiting, with the crowd nervous of interaction and some self-consciously distancing themselves from some parent or other oblivious to the fact they shouldn't have been there at all. Other than that it was a mixed lot, some of them who looked like parents actually enrolling mature-age students as nervous as the teenagers. That's what gave them away and helped the others relax.

Peter put on his grandfather's impassive desert face and stood inert, waiting, while Alex paced about worrying over Sam's skeletal film footage and what could be done about fleshing it out, and making it into something worth his name.

Eventually he became aware of another student standing there watching him, a classically handsome boy with dark curly hair, soft brown eyes, and a thoughtful, watchful look about him. He stopped to return the gaze. The other frowned briefly and stepped forward.

"You are bound to him like you're on a leash," the boy said, indicating Peter. "I notice you've been circling him at a distance of almost exactly one metre for the past ten minutes, like you're the dog and he's the post, and the chain is only so long, do you realise that?"

"What?"

A girl with long blond hair and a sunny smile stepped up and took the other's arm, glancing quickly at Alex as she tried leading him away.

"Asperger's," she said over her shoulder.

"Don't say that, Sair. Stop it, we're past all that. We're here now. We made it finally. I can be friends with anyone I want, can't I?" the boy said.

"It's not Asperger's anyway," another boy also blond who might have been her brother said from behind, grinning broadly, "he's an adrenaline junkie with an IQ through the roof, way up there in the clouds, and can't help himself."

"Yes, Sair, stop it; you too Robert." Another girl stepped up, just as beautiful but with black hair, high cheeks and dark eyes almost Spanish, or gypsy.

She looked intently at Alex. "This is Nicolas, he writes plays among other gifted things he does. It's just the way he looks at people, the way he sees things."

Nicolas stood there, smiling, wide eyed like a little boy. Then he stepped up and held out his hand.

"I'm Nicolas Bruic, pronounced 'Brook' not 'Brick' or 'Break', as some headmasters would have it, who are no longer with us," he announced. "And this is my wife, the lovely Emma, and my next lovely wife Sarah, and behind us there, the comedian, is Robbie, who's a drop-dead spunk in his own right. He's the other husband, besides me, four of all altogether, all married. Neat, eh?"

Alex frowned and turned away, and touching Peter's elbow to follow stepped into the office after the queue. The four of them followed close behind, smiling intently, not saying anything. They stood close together as if there were nothing between them, and Alex realised they must have come in a group.

They came to the long bench against the wall and following the little signs began taking the relevant forms to fill them in with the pens provided. That done they moved along and handed them across the counter, then stood waiting for their names to be called.

Finally Alex heard his name and stepped forward for his enrolment certificate, but as he turned from the counter he bumped into Nicolas standing close behind him.

"Ah! Now, I know who you are," the other said. "Alexander Anthony

John Lennox. You're the rich Melbourne kid who disappeared a few years back and everyone went looking for you, after you were caught fucking your Dad's hell hot chickie-babe in his bed and thought you were going to be arrested for it. And now you're over here in WA - big mistake, or maybe not. We have a lot in common. Also you're doing Anthropology and English, same as me."

Alex stood there stunned. They were all looking at him, especially Peter, watching his face. Then Sarah leaned forward and kissed his cheek, pressing her whole body against his while the others beamed. Then Emma gave him a full body hug likewise.

"We'd better find someone for you, so you won't be lonely. And your friend."

"What? No, wait a minute, he's married already. He has a wife up at Warmunya, tribally anyway."

They were interrupted as Peter's name was called, then the others in quick succession, so without waiting for a reply Alex took his chance to escape and wait outside. He hadn't come here expecting this. That Nicolas was right, he had run away after being found in bed with the drop-dead gorgeous Ysabella, one of his Dad's second-puberty girlfriends, and it was in all the newspapers, but that was back when he was a Jedi Master and called himself Obi Wan Kenobi, back when he was twelve, before he ran into Sam, and Peter.

Now he was somebody, grownup nearly, his own man, and 2,000 miles away. He'd set up the company structure, pegged out and developed a gold mine in the meantime, and designed a now priceless set of presentation jewellery using opals and sapphires he'd secretly inherited from old George Summers, the cranky Queensland prospector killed by a King Brown snake up in the Central Desert. But shit, that was a lifetime ago, another book in his life altogether.

At that moment Robbie came out of the crowded office and said gently, "Don't worry about them, they're nuts. We'll catch up sometime, all right?"

He turned and gazed at him a moment then softened and nodded. "OK, catch up. See you around."

As he looked up Peter was there so he swung around and back up the path toward the road and bus stop. He decided then that they might go into the city and look around, and meet Sam later for lunch maybe, or simply go home when they were ready. He didn't realise they'd be late, and in no mood for relaxed chat when they finally got home.

Chapter Seven

The 102 bus into the city dropped them off in Barrack Street and they crossed back over to the Supreme Court Gardens to have a look around. There were a few big old Queensland Bunya pines there, two of which had dropped their huge nut-filled cones that lay broken and scattered about. Alex picked up a few nuts and put them in his pocket, expecting a snack when he got home, but apart from that there was nothing much of interest. There was a funny looking faux-modernist building next door that housed the city council. Along the street to the west, past great expanses of dry lawn on the one hand and strangely out-of-place, pretentious, colonial brick buildings on the other, another new building was going up in much the same style.

It was shady along there under the huge Moreton Bay figs, however, so they went that way and turning right came up onto St George's Terrace by a laneway against the flow of one-way traffic. On the Terrace they headed west again, across William Street, past a grubby sandstone newspaper building, a public trustee building in the same style, and an old church-looking place that advertised itself as the original Perth Boys School, until beyond that point it was all new buildings going up. There was a decrepit residential building there with protest banners along the front complaining about people being evicted from the city, until right at the end there was a lone brick archway from which freeway traffic noise came at them in a dull persistent roar.

Across the street an interesting façade advertised itself as The Atrium and they crossed over to have a look. Inside was a high day-lit open space with offices along balconies up to their left, and a great three storey water wall to the right. Alex gazed about, thinking this place must be the first unselfconscious space he'd found here, except there was no interconnection with anything else, or sense of belonging.

He turned to Peter who simply shrugged before indicating a tiny exit up a short ramp. He wasn't impressed either.

Exiting through a set of automatic glass doors they came out into a bare tiled corridor that led eventually to some shops and finally out onto Hay Street.

Standing on the verge gazing about the two boys noticed a crowd gathered across the road, near an old brick church on the corner. They headed that way and as they drew close checked the traffic and, road clear for two hundred metres either way, crossed over to join the throng.

As they did so a policeman stepped out of the crowd and approached them.

"Do you realise you've crossed against the lights?" he demanded to know.

"What? The lights are way over there, and the road was clear. We wanted to see what the fuss was, what the crowd was looking at."

"Smartarse, are ya? All right, wait here."

Twenty minutes later as the crowd dispersed, tickets in hand and complaining loudly, the boys were left waiting their turn.

"What's yer name, mate?"

"Why do I have to give you my name? We haven't done anything."

"Just give it to me, stop giving us the shits. We've had a hard day."

"Alexander Lennox, and this is Peter Napantjarra. Peter Wilson Napantjarra."

The cop flicked his chin quickly to his mate who started talking on his radio handset, then turning the page on his notepad started writing.

As he finished the first page and handed Alex a $20 ticket for jaywalking within 20 metres of a red-lit pedestrian sign his partner came over and said, "Alexander Anthony Lennox, is that correct?"

"Alexander Anthony John Lennox."

"Smart cunt," he paused, eyeing him, before nodding to himself. "Whatever way you want it, mate, I don't give a shit."

He looked up, officially, "I require you to accompany me to the nearest police station for questioning. We have reason to suspect you may be a serial sex offender and may have been implicated in the death of one George Summers north of Alice Springs in 1986, and in the theft of a quantity of gemstones."

He turned to Peter.

"I require you also to accompany me to the nearest police station for questioning about the near-fatal spearing of one Francis Aloysius Lacy north of Alice Springs in 1986, in which we have reason to suspect you may have been implicated."

By then his partner had finished writing the second jaywalking ticket and handed it to Peter, who simply shrugged and glancing only briefly at Alex turned to follow.

Alex propped, going nowhere.

"We don't have to go anywhere with you. That business was years ago, and cleared by the magistrate in Tennant Creek as death by misadventure. I was still a child, and didn't know what to do. I tried to save him. Peter was only a child too, just turned twelve. We were awarded ownership of George's truck while Dr Sam Flanagan with Peter here was given the reward for finding me. That reward money was posted by my father. I was lost in the desert, that was all, and nearly died of exposure. Those people up there saved my life. We don't know anything else. As far as I can tell Frank Lacy was George's old prospecting partner, but we never had anything to do with him. I want a lawyer."

The policeman eyed him up and down, and winked at his partner.

"All right, if that's what you want. You can ring your lawyer in due course. Right now I'm arresting you for loitering, and obstructing the course of justice."

"You can't do that. We weren't loitering, you pulled us up."

"Watch us. We have the power to restrain you and call for backup. You can come along peacefully, or we can take you with whatever force is reasonable in the circumstances. You'll have to explain your refusal to the magistrate. Do you understand that, or do I have to repeat myself?"

Alex stood shaking his head in anger and frustration, but Peter's expressionless face and relaxed body language caused him to follow nonetheless as they turned to leave.

Parked at the end of the block was a police wagon. The passing crowd cast guilty glances in their direction as they were ushered into the back of the wagon, or walked on by staring fixedly ahead.

Ten minutes or so they were bundled out again and herded inside a tall faux-modernist building like the council chambers, but without the checkered exterior cladding, and shoved downstairs into a holding cell. They were ordered to strip while one officer went through their clothing and arranged the contents of their pockets on a bench. The other donned a surgical glove and indicated for Alex to step forward. After a brisk frontal once-over he reached down and fondled him, lifting his scrotum for inspection. He then made him turn around and bend over while he examined him from the rear. Alex felt a finger inserted in his anus and joggled about before being removed, and then he was turned around and fondled again. Discarding the used glove and pulling on a new one the man gave Peter the same treatment.

"Standard procedure, son. Drug search. You can never be too careful these days," he said.

The full body search over, they were allowed to dress before being taken upstairs again to an office and fingerprinted and their mug shots taken. While their personal details were being taken one of the officers went through their university enrolment papers.

"Ah, University students, are you? Not going to have any trouble from you, are we?"

"Why would we give you trouble?" Alex said blankly. His feathers were seriously ruffled, his face as taut and eyes glazed and unseeing as Peter's. "We only arrived yesterday, and we wanted to see the city. We went over to the University to enroll - there are our papers - then we took a 102 bus into town. We hadn't been here more than about 20 minutes. Nice bloody welcome to Perth, eh?"

"Enough from you, son; it's our job to keep the city safe. Pay your fines at the Central Law Courts, sooner the better. If you don't there'll be costs, and in default a couple of days in jail. Be warned, and keep your nose clean."

As they were about to leave the policeman asked, "Still want that lawyer?"

"Are you still making enquiries?"

"What do you reckon? You stupid or something? We have an understanding, do we?"

Alex stopped, gazing off into the distance as if the walls had ceased to be. He nodded to himself before turning slowly away.

"You might say that," he said on the way out.

Chapter Eight

When Sam arrived home they were both in bed asleep.

Alex as soon as he'd got in the door went into the tiny bathroom and vomited in the toilet, then washed his mouth out in the basin. Stripping completely he left his clothes on the floor and stepped into the shower and scrubbed himself all over, paying special attention to his backside. When he got out he realised their towels were hanging over the feet of their beds so he walked through wet and dripping, took Peter's towel and threw it to him then brusquely dried himself with his own. Peter likewise walked through wet from the shower, not looking for his towel which he'd picked up anyway from the bathroom floor, merely wanting to stay in contact.

Sam's mood was upbeat and he came in with a spring in his step, but when he saw Alex curled up under the sheet like a foetus, and Peter lying there face close to the wall, the place deathly quiet, he sensed something was badly awry.

He sat on Alex's bed and touched him on the shoulder to wake him but he winced and drew away, so he went out again and put some good Country and Western music on with the volume down. Stopping in the middle of the room he turned suddenly, and went out and across the road to the bottle shop where he bought a six-pack of beer. Crossing back over the road he checked the mailbox on afterthought to find a fine parchment envelope there addressed to Alex, post-marked Weilmoragi, NSW, and forwarded from Toorak post office with a modern, urgent *par avion* sticker that rather spoiled its presentation.

Inside again he peeked into the boy's room to see Peter on his back, and Alex peeping from under the sheet.

"What's up, boys?"

Alex sat up tossing the sheet off, then bent down to pick up his underpants and slipped them on.

"Nothing," he said. "We'll sort it."

"Not going to tell me?"

"No."

Alex pushed his way past into the living room and saw the six-pack on the breakfast bar.

"Got some beer, eh? Go and get some more, a carton, I'll give you the money."

Sam looked steadily at him. He nodded, "No, save it. My shout."

On the way out the door he turned and said, "Letter for you."

Alex glanced down as Sam disappeared out the door, leaning forward curiously to take in the fine parchment with its beautiful calligraphy, and Auntie Edie's shaky, arthritic copperplate overwriting her Toorak address with his new Perth address. He fingered it a moment, turning it over to find a return address, but there was nothing apart from the original Weilmoragi franking stamp.

He left it there and went back into their room to pull on a pair of crumpled shorts from their clean laundry, and a loose cotton shirt. He sat on the edge of his bed waiting for Peter to stir, and when he did said simply, "Sam's getting us a carton."

Peter gazed at him intently with his dark impenetrable eyes, his face a mask, until Alex nodded almost to himself and went out. Peter sat up in bed and leaned forward to examine himself, until satisfied he stood and dressed, like Alex, from the clean laundry basket.

In the living room Alex was standing over the letter on Sam's desk, but when Peter came out he looked away and stepping over to the bar pulled a cold stubby from the plastic wrapper and handed it to him. At that moment Sam arrived back with a full carton and setting it on the bench cracked it open and started packing the fridge.

"Um, good news," he said finally, taking a stubby for himself. "What about coming out to Barkhan Crossing with me for the weekend? Somebody I want you to meet."

No response. The two boys were staring at the old-fashioned letter on the desk, like something from somebody's ancestral hall it seemed, until finally Peter said quietly, "That Little Artie boy looking at you."

Alex glanced at him, ignoring Sam. He stood suddenly and taking up the letter on the way past went into their room and shut the door. Sitting on the bed he turned it over, and over again, looking at it. He put it on his bedside table and stood to go out to get his beer, but turned around and sat again on the bed. He picked up the letter, fingering the fine parchment and exquisitely lettered calligraphy, wondering who on earth might have sent it to him. He tapped his forehead with it, and finally slipping his thumb under the red wax seal tore it open. Taking out the single parchment he read:

Talaria Station

Private Mail Bag

Weilmoragi, NSW

10th February

Dear Alexander,

I write to apologise for my rudeness in not coming out to farewell you at the end of your visit. Mother said it was unbecoming of me. But I am only a country boy and you are a legend. You shine. I hope I will see you again and you can tell me things.

Great-grandmother Elizabeth allowed me to use some of her nice writing paper to correspond with you while we are all still here on Eurongera, but it is my handwriting. She teaches me calligraphy.

My other hobbies are saddlery, landscape painting and leather carving, and I also do emu eggs. I am learning how to make this lovely fine paper, and red wax seals, but it is all a bit too complicated yet. I hope you like my work.

I attend the Mount Jambla Grammar School during the year, where I am in Year 7. You may write to me there. You will know the address.

I love you, Alex.

Your best friend in the world,
Arthur Andrew Edward MacFarlane, Esq.
of Talaria, Dadjari, and Eurongera.

When Sam came in twenty minutes later looking for him, Alex was back under the top sheet, the letter under his pillow.

When he was stirred this time he stood abruptly and went out, and picking up his warm half-drank stubby tipped it down the sink and took a cold one from the fridge. He sat down.

"Sam," he said, "You're a Flanagan, so you understand a thing or two, except from the Irish side, across the water, is that right?"

He shrugged, looking away into the distance, adding as afterthought, "we wouldn't be here otherwise, together, us."

Without waiting for an answer he went on, "If you understand things, sort of, maybe you will see the old Scottish Clan MacFarlane were retainers to the Earls of Lennox, way back then."

Peter's eyes glinted, smiling inwardly, but Sam simply listened, and waited.

Eventually he looked up and said, "And I'm a Lennox, and those boys out on Eurongera are MacFarlanes. Is there a race memory, do you think?"

"Don't worry about this mob," he added, indicating Peter. "I mean, it's separate."

Sam stood and went to the fridge for another beer for himself and Peter. Passing one over he opened his own and said, "I don't think anything about it, Alex. I've been doing Anthropology too long, and all this is undergraduate stuff. If you want an answer from me you need to open up about whatever else is going on, otherwise I can't help you."

The boys stared at him, and remained silent.

Sam sipped his beer, and relaxed and turned around. He sat in his chair and leaned forward.

"What I wanted to tell you about, when I came home, is after this morning I went over to the Anthropology Department to look up some old colleagues, and seek advice. They said go out and have a yarn with Bill Hanna, out at Barkhan Crossing. What I really only wanted to know, when I came in, is do you want to come for a drive this weekend?"

Peter answered first, "Yeah, no worries. Have a look around, eh?"

Chapter Nine

It was quite different here under the towering trees than being out in the desert. The mood of the great southwest forest was soft, lingering, hypnotic. Mere shafts of sunlight penetrated the dense canopy high above. The air hummed with tiny insects darting about, flashing as they passed through vertical sunbeams, and thick undergrowth obliged walkers to stay on the track. It was cool, too, despite the hot day.

The anthropologist they'd come to see was away. They'd missed him by half an hour and he wouldn't be back until tomorrow. While Sam went off on some other business Alex and Peter decided to go for a walk along the river, but had separated in the thick bush.

Walking on Alex soon heard the rush of water over rocks below. He was tired and glad of the distraction so he made his way down the long slope until he came to a small overflowing weir where he took off his boots and socks to sit, feet dangling in the cool pond.

Since they'd camped on those lakes off Eurongera Station he hadn't had a moment to himself. It wasn't that it had been arduous or intrusive, quite the opposite, once their station hands had brought the stock horses down and they rode the rest of the way leaving their vehicles with the stockmen to manage.

It was amazing the way everybody in their party had taken to the saddle, even the small boys as if they'd been born to it, and when they all arrived rode right in past the big homestead like they did in the old days, in their fine saddles and gear to a thunder of hooves. He chuckled as he thought of it. Kick arse, those old fellas, knew how to impress, and make a statement.

But then there was Little Artie sleeping next to his bed, constantly shadowing him, hanging onto him for dear life. He kicked himself for not paying him enough attention, fobbing him off as just a kid, when it was he who'd made those beautifully carved leather place mats for the big dining table, and the fine portraits carved into the emu eggs along the mantle below the gun rack, that he'd thought were just part of the old place.

That's what Peter had been trying to say to him. He was treating those boys the same way he'd been treated to that age, rattling around the big house in Toorak by himself all these years when he should have been allowed his childhood, until finally at 12 he'd started fooling around with one of his father's fancy girlfriends, and got caught and run away. Those Eurongera boys had serious talent and solid values in life. No wonder they all held to each other the way they did.

Then the long flight down to Melbourne and meetings with Ned Collins and Aunty Edie, who chatted intimately and incessantly like they were brother and sister as they set up their new joint scholarship fund for outback children. He'd watched them both closely. They were real polished diamonds under their day-to-day working façade, not rough at all, with their lovely old Victorian English when they put their minds to it; almost misfits in today's world, yet entirely adaptable to their surroundings, old colonial stock who still knew what it meant to have good manners, and sit at table on starched white linen, and know who you are. No wonder Angus still carried his odd lilting accent and cavalry pose, despite the crick in his neck and his strange ways.

The old boy had given him a quick clip under the ear as a reminder when he made to comment, yet tousled his hair as they parted, then turned away and left without a word.

After that it was across to Perth against that perpetual headwind, and the bullshit since.

A hot breeze stirred the surface of the water making it glisten in the sunlight, but then he heard Peter calling him so he dried his feet with his shirt and pulling his socks and boots back on made his way back up to the walk trail.

Halfway up the cry sharpened, and he glanced up suddenly sniffing the breeze, and then began to run, crashing through the undergrowth.

Back up on the track Peter was lying on the ground with some boys standing over him.

They backed away sullen as he approached. They hadn't expected anyone else to be around it seemed; much less a tall, rangy youth in moleskins with a bearing and purpose.

One of them came forward as he approached.

"Sorry," the boy said, a bit too quickly. "He tripped and fell over. We're helpin' him up."

When they got back up to the caravan park Peter went directly across for a shower. He had something of a long bruise on his middle back extending to his left buttock, and his hip was grazed and bleeding. When Alex followed him in saw him there with his back to a wall mirror, shoulders twisted around and head down, trying to see the extent of it.

"What did they do?" he wanted to know.

"Bit of that whitefella parody, I reckon, sense of bloody humour."

"What did they do, smartarse?"

"Nothin'! Shut up about it."

So Alex said nothing. As they showered he helped Peter clean himself up, washed off the sand and gravel from the dirt track, those parts he couldn't reach, or see properly without the mirror, and then gently patted his back dry with the towel before drying himself. Peter's nice trousers were ruined but he slipped them back on and walked back to the cabin with his towel over his shoulder.

"There's a new cultural centre being built around here somewhere," Sam said when they got back to the cabin. "You boys want to go for a drive this arvo, have a look at the place?"

"What's that?" Peter wanted to know.

"Cultural centre, I know where it is, up on the old coast road toward that big cape, back this way a bit from the lighthouse," Alex piped in.

"Nah, nothing," Peter insisted; "can't build bloody cultural centre. Can't build culture, in a place, put up a building, is it. Culture already there, from old time, in the land, can't build it."

Sam watched them, pausing for a moment. "We'll go and have a look, eh? We can take the cameras, and ask them what's going on; that's better, don't you think?"

Alex dropped his towel and started dressing. "Maybe it's an idea," he said thoughtfully. He glanced up at Peter. "At least we can talk to them and find out what's happening."

"Yeah, all right, no worries," the other shrugged, and turned to pull on underpants.

Already clothed and ready to go Sam stepped out onto the small porch to wait. It was beautiful here right on the river but the cabins were tiny with barely enough room to swing the one cat, much less two boundless bush adolescents. It would be good to sit here of an evening with a cold beer, going over his day's filming, but there was something wrong. He missed the enormity of the desert; this was new country entirely, new people, and he had to stop blaming himself.

"Alex, you ready yet? Want to ask you something," he turned and said.

"What?"

"What's wrong with this place, do you reckon?"

No answer came so he leaned forward to glance back through the screen door. The boys were both there looking out at him, abashed. Peter had changed his trousers and put on a clean shirt, turning to the mirror to comb his hair. When he was done he came out onto the porch while Alex finished tidying himself.

"What's up?" he wanted to know.

Sam looked away across the cut grass and water, and forest beyond, and abruptly back again, without saying anything.

Peter exchanged looks with him and frowned.

"Bit claustrophobic this place, eh? Opened up only little bit. Funny, you know, like magic, got two sides, something good something bad. Forest country, yeah?"

"Do you think that's what it is?"

"What are you thinking about, Sam?" Alex interjected. "I mean, why are you asking?"

"There's death here, a lot of it. The place is spooked by it. Watch people's faces, when you get a chance; the way they stop and stare, like they are all trying to hide something, or protect something, or maybe themselves from something."

He was frustrated, he knew. The university job in Perth wasn't working out the way he'd thought it would. He didn't like being supervised and edited all the time, having to crop all the footage and warned off; treading constantly on egg-shells. It was the same there, except here in the southwest forest the feeling was so much more intense.

Finally he sighed and got up, and turned to look at the boys standing there.

"I think I'll throw the job in. I'm uncomfortable with it. We don't need the money. Better to simply branch out as an independent." He glanced at them, then away into the distance.

Chapter Ten

The narrow winding coast road took a lot of concentration and they nearly missed the turnoff. They'd driven through fairly open coastal heathland interspersed with deeply shaded stands of Peppermint and occasional Melaleuca where it was swampy, but here on a ridge the dense Marri and Jarrah woodland with its heavy understory of karri hazel and high clumping grass obscured their line of sight.

Coming around a tight u-bend the road sign was there suddenly, and Sam pulled up in time only because Peter was onto it.

Once they were off the main road Alex leaned forward and tapped him on the shoulder. "Sam, can I drive?" he wanted to know.

Sam thought for a moment then pulled over. He looked across at Peter and suggested he sit in the back so he could keep an eye on Alex while he was behind the wheel, and the three got out and swapped around. Alex wasn't a bad driver and they got away clean. After all he had driven hundreds of miles across the Central Desert at the age of twelve in a big old Landcruiser with a dead body in the back, and had plenty of time to think about it since. That was only a little over five years ago.

Before long they came out into the open again, and could see a rooftop through a grove of Peppermint trees. There was a rustic post-and-rail fence and a sandy gravel driveway, with not much in the way of lawn or even grass, just bare ground, so they turned in and drove up to a small car park marked out by cut logs and stopped. Nobody there apparently, they got out and had a look around.

The big rammed earth building had a low roof, like a big old country hall with a wide side veranda extending about three metres out, under which were scattered rough-sawn trestle tables and wooden benches. Alex went up to a window and looked through, and turned and shrugged. He was about to say something when a brown snowy-haired old man came limping around the end of the building. The old fellow stopped in his tracks, frowning, staring intently at Peter, then glancing at Sam and Alex smiled a greeting.

"How ya goin'," he said in a slow drawl, "Doin' all right are ya?"

"Yeah, good," Sam replied. "Thought we'd come out and look the place over. We saw your brochure at the Tourist Bureau."

"Right you are, then," the other nodded. "Make yer a cuppa tea if ya like, that suit ya?"

"We were looking for the indigenous cultural centre; we thought we might be at the wrong place," Alex said.

"Nah, this is it. Get a crowd here sometimes, when the boys come up with their dancing and we 'ave a bit of a corroboree. Show 'em a bit a bush tucker, spear-throwin', boomerangs and the like; play the didge, song sticks. French people love it, Germans too, eh? Not so sure about those Danish bastards, or Pommie Englishmen, few of the others. Brazilians all right, come here for the surf, eh? Like to party, fair dinkum. Real nice sheilas they got, those fellas."

The old man stopped suddenly, staring again at Peter.

"Where you from, son?" he wanted to know.

Peter glared back, eyes narrowed.

"We've been working up in the Central Desert, and came across to Perth on a job." Sam interjected. "This is Peter Wilson Napantjarra. His grandfather is Bertram Napantjarra, the chief lawman for the Warmunya community."

He turned to Alex. "And this is Alexander Lennox, who is also studying Aboriginal traditional law. He's doing first year literature and anthropology at university. My name is Sam Flanagan; I'm an anthropologist and film-maker. These boys are with me."

The other nodded, and turned away

He turned back again, defiant. "Different country here, mate, different planet, eh? Our people warred with that desert mob, long time ago. Then the bloody stupid whitefella came along and fucked everything completely. Didn't they, eh? Poor old black bastard couldn't see the enemy, could 'e, eh, till it was too late." He shook his head sadly, gazing off into the distance before turning to Alex.

"Like the old blackfella, do yer, mate?"

Alex frowned, and cocked his head. "No, not always, some of them are real deadshits, got no time for them. Same as whitefellas, ratty they are, bloody coconuts."

He waited for a rejoinder but none came.

"Anyway," he went on after a long pause, "Peter's not a blackfella; he's a proper black bastard, a real cunt, I know that for a fact, blacker than you, eh? And he's my tribal brother, properly, same skin, so that makes me a proper black bastard too."

He reached sideways and shoved Peter, who shoved back, grinning.

"Well, that's the way it is then," the old man said finally. "Come inside an' 'ave a cuppa tea, eh?"

With a slow sigh he led the way through the big hall to a small kitchen at the back. He had a billy on the stove, not a kettle, and rummaging around found bread and butter, and a jar of jam.

Chapter Eleven

As they drove back up the low ridge, along the dirt track and back onto the old coast road, Sam said thoughtfully, "You boys happy with going to Uni?"

They glanced at one another and shrugged. "All right," Peter said, "no worries. School's bloody school, eh? Same everywhere. We haven't started yet, properly."

He said nothing for a moment, until Alex replied, "That's not what you want to know, Sam, is it. Just say what you're thinking about, it's okay, we're with you."

"Well, I don't want you to start fucking around, if we move again."

"We don't fuck around. Anyway, it's not your business is it? Auntie Edie's the boss not you, and Bertram, and now Mr Collins; that Eurongera mob. Just say what you want to say, Sam."

"Don't get smart, mate, because legally you're in my care and I'm answerable."

Peter glanced sharply across, "You big brother, all right, not grandfather. Not the same. You look after us, no worries. We like you, properly. That brother, Alecki, you save his life, he love you, everything. Proper little brother for you, that boy, show big respect for you, eh? What you talking about?"

Sam drove on a while before answering, "Sorry boys; wrong question. That's not what I meant. What I mean is I'd like to move down here and chase up this local mob, and find out what's going on. I'm not sure if I can get any real filming done, like we did at Puntayeri, but there's a lot of research to be done here. Nobody seems to want to do it, for some reason, and I'd like to know about that too. I'm not happy with things over here at all."

There was silence for the next kilometre or so, but after they reached the road and headed south again Alex said simply, "What you mean is they won't fund your research; what you want to do. Is that right? They want you working on their pet projects, don't they?"

"Hhmmm," Sam replied thoughtfully. "You shouldn't be worrying about that, mate. You're a first year student and you really need to concentrate on learning your theory and method before you start saying anything like that to anyone."

"But it's true, isn't it. Aunty Edie is always on about it. That's why she likes you."

Sam sighed, not saying anything.

"So," Alex persisted, "that being the reason I say no, we're not leaving. I don't agree with you, Sam. We need to stay settled for a while and we need you with us."

"How long have we been together now?" he went on. "Five years or more, is it? We're good together, we're a team."

"OK, OK, sorry I mentioned it," Sam said finally. "You're right; I'm just frustrated with the whole business, that's all."

Chapter Twelve

By time they got back to their cabin at the camping park Sam was fidgety. His instinct that something wasn't quite right in the district didn't help much, but at the same time he was also worried about the long bruise on Peter's back, that he didn't want to talk about. The boys were starting to hold too much back, he thought; perhaps he should have gone across to Eurongera with them but he really had too much on his plate. They were young men now, with tertiary entry scores that would get them into any university in Australia, and he had to respect that.

"Lighten up a bit, Sam," Alex interrupted his thoughts.

He looked up, "Yeah, sorry boys. What would you like to do? It's still early."

"Might go for a walk up the street, eh? There's a cool breeze now and not so hot. We can take a look around town, see if there's a half-decent restaurant somewhere."

Peter hung back. "*Mupan* here. No good this place."

Alex turned to him, exasperated. "We'll go and find out, what do you reckon? I'm not going to hang around here, stuck in this tiny little cabin, that's for sure."

He went to go out the door then paused, thinking a moment.

"We'll stay together, OK? Sorry we got separated this morning, we didn't realise. But we agreed to meet up across the bend in the river, didn't we. I was waiting for you where I said I would, but it didn't turn out. Then I went back and got you straight away, didn't I."

He turned and went out; holding the door open while Peter and Sam trooped past, then he jumped off the steps and led the way back up the narrow road toward town. After about ten paces he slowed so they'd be together, but nobody said anything. The road was overhung and shady at this end, and opened up into cleared land then residential blocks as they drew close to the main street.

No sooner had they emerged onto the main road and turned toward the shopping centre when a police wagon pulled up beside them, and two officers stepped out and approached them.

"Been looking for you," one said, somewhat abruptly.

The two boys held back slightly while Sam stepped forward.

"I'm Dr Flanagan. Can I help?"

The policeman eyed him curiously before dismissing him, "No, it's the boys we're after. Seems there was a bit of a scuffle this morning and we've received a complaint. Mightn't be anything, you know how it is, but you can't be too careful, can you."

Sam turned in askance, but Alex simply shrugged. "Not us. Wrong guys, we don't even know what he's talking about. This morning we went for a walk along the river, and we came back. That was it."

"Didn't meet up with anyone?"

"What? No, not a soul. What are you talking about?"

At that moment, before the policeman could reply, an old farm truck with P-plates front and back pulled up and Nicolas, the odd boy they'd met at university the day before waved at them gaily from the driver's window.

"Alexander!"

"Nicolas, what? What are you doing here?"

Nicolas looked taken aback, disappointed almost, then eyeing the two policeman got out and said, "Ah, yes, sorry I'm late, thought you might be able to find your way but we waited and waited for you. Thought I'd better come in and see where you'd got to."

He shook his hand, and turned to the policeman and said, "Sorry,

Constable Peters, they're with me, guests for the weekend."

He turned back and said, a little too quickly, "Get in; I'll give you a lift."

Sam and Peter got in the front by the passenger door, and Nicolas looked back over his shoulder at the policemen, standing there nonplussed. "Don't mind if Alex gets in the back?"

Without waiting for a reply Alex jumped in the back of the truck and Nicolas got back into the driver's seat and made a quick U-turn there on the street.

"You seriously do not want to know those two guys," he said. "Tell me where you're staying."

Sam leaned forward slightly and looking past Peter said, "Sorry, young fella, I don't have a clue who you are. Would you like to tell me what's going on? We came down this weekend to see an anthropologist by the name of Bill Hanna, but he's away until tomorrow, apparently. I'm Dr Sam Flanagan."

"What? Bill? No, he's not away he's out at our place. Want to see him, do you? I'll take you out. Where are you staying?"

"Caravan Park," Peter said.

"Oh, shit, back there. Fuck, um, OK, hang on."

Two hundred metres along the road Nicolas turned left suddenly onto an unmade side track. He slowed before negotiating two tight bends past the town rubbish tip and came back quickly onto the narrow road to the caravan park. As they drove back in through the main gate Sam pointed out the third cabin on their right and he pulled up in a cloud of dust.

"Get your stuff, you're staying with us, OK. Don't argue. How much did you pay for this dump? Why didn't you ring, shit, we'd put you up. Fucking rip-off merchants."

By this time Alex was standing at the driver's window. "What the bloody hell are you doing? Who on earth are you, and what are you doing way out here? What the fuck's going on?"

"Ah, Alexander, the Great, you survived!" Nicolas said, startled, looking at him. "Yes, um, this is where we live, didn't you know? I mean, not here, not in town, out a bit. I thought maybe you'd come to visit us, when I saw you. But then, you hadn't called, except you were being nailed by Marchant and Peters of all cops, so you cannot possibly be an enemy of ours, you can only be friends. OK, by corollary, you're staying with us. This town is, I mean, seriously not a good place to be. It's like, fucked, really. Put your gear in the back and I'll take it."

Peter caught his eye and nodded. Nicolas smiled in satisfaction.

He turned to Sam.

"Bill's out with us right now, at our place, something came up. I mean, there's the connection, really, I hadn't made it before now. He said a colleague was arriving sometime over the weekend that he wanted to meet, a film-maker, and that's you, isn't it. Somebody'd rung him from the university, to say you were coming. OK, now we're sorted. I can see what's happening. Put your gear in the back and I'll take it, you follow me, all right?"

Alex stood there dazed, disoriented by the sudden turn of events, and change of pace.

Finally he said, "All right. Um, Pete, you want to go with Sam in the Landcruiser? I want to talk to this guy. He's got an idea I'm some sort of legend but I don't know him from a bar of soap."

"What, another one?" Peter answered dryly.

Chapter Thirteen

The old place they drove up to after a drive of about 10 miles was huge rambling limestone and wide verandas heavily overgrown with Hardenbergia creeper covering half the front of the house. Remnants of uncut lawn and old rose bushes straggling to form a hedge amongst the kikuyu left worn foot-beaten tracks up to the front porch. A few sheep wandered about, keeping things more or less in trim. Along one side against the setting sun was a tall shady bamboo grove, equally unkempt.

Nicolas drove the truck into a nearby shed and getting out waited for Alex, then taking his shopping from the back led him past a big old fig tree that had been blasted in half by lightning, by the look of it, through a huge glass conservatory into the kitchen. Inside it was dim; cool with an old, dry, musty, lived-in smell like the place hadn't been aired in over fifty years, but with vibrant overtones of youth and music. There were quite a few people sitting around the big table, drinking beer and taking quietly among themselves.

They looked up as the boys entered.

"Look what I've found!" Nicolas announced breathlessly, putting the shopping on the table. "The famous Alexander, except he said not to call him that, so don't, OK."

Just then he pricked his ears up and rushed outside again, calling out to somebody, and a minute later returned with Sam and Peter in tow.

"Bill," he said, "this is Sam Flanagan, who was in town looking for you."

A solid, well-built, medium height bloke in bush clothes with a flowing white beard and kindly weather-beaten face stood and extended his hand.

"Ah, we meet finally," he said in a booming though modulated voice. "It's my pleasure, Dr Flanagan, we've heard a lot about you."

He turned to Peter first and shook hands, then Alex, and turning back to the table started shuffling chairs to make room for them.

Before they sat he started introducing the others, Emma and Sarah who they'd already met, and Robbie, then Sarah's father Karl, and beside him Professor Marcus Trent-Brown, and his partner Liz who turned out to be Robbie's mother. Alex started noticing the resemblances, and when it came to Jennie at the end of the table he realised she could only possibly be Emma's mother. She had two five year-olds with her, twins, a boy and a girl every bit as handsome as Emma. Two more boys came barging in at that point, 11-12 year-old twins this time, quite as handsome and well-built, hair wet and dripping naked from playing under the sprinkler but curious about the new arrivals. Nobody paid them any attention, until satisfied they disappeared again.

There was cold beer on the table with snacks, and the moment they were seated glasses were poured and platters of food passed across, with smiles all round.

"OK," Sam said finally. "Fill us in will you. What's happening?"

Bill nodded.

"To cut a long story short, what's happening is the government a while back declared a tough on crime policy and the shithead cops are having a field day. Nothing superficially wrong with that, but now we have a spate of teenage suicides on our hands."

"The police are corrupt," Nicolas broke in, interrupting. "and now the drugs have moved in . . ."

He stopped, glancing accusingly across at Karl and Marcus.

"What I mean is," he went on, "hard drugs and serious dealers, and the cops we have here now are in on it. So they're being real cunts."

Sam cocked his head thoughtfully, and then looked up at Alex.

Alex caught his expression and sat back. He gazed around the room and back at him, his face intense, and eyes glistening.

"They stripped us, when we were in the city," he said quietly, after a long pause, "and fondled our dick and balls, and stuck their finger up our arse doing a 'drug check', so they said. But it was only to humiliate us, and intimidate us, not just me but Peter. They didn't do a breath test, or take blood samples, or anything you'd expect."

He sank back into himself while Peter sat there impassive, until Jennie leaned forward and placing her hand over his said quietly, "It's all right, Alex, you're among friends. We've been through all this."

Sam glanced at her, then at Alex, watching his face. He leaned forward.

"What is it, Bill?" he wanted to know.

"Turf war, I reckon."

Chapter Fourteen

The young people eventually bored of the discussion, amounting almost to a council of war at some points, and started glancing at one another. Sarah kept looking at Nicolas, until ignored by him stood and removed her summer frock and sat down again in only her panties. Then she stood again and removed them as well. Nobody said anything, except Alex smiled only slightly before focusing back on the conversation.

"You're not going to hook him like that, Sair," Nicolas blurted out suddenly, at which Jenny looked up, annoyed, and said, "Children, some decorum please, else just bugger off will you?"

She turned to Emma.

"Em, why don't you take your friends and show them around? They'll have to stay with you up at Edoras, we have no room here. Dr Flanagan can have the extra bed in the old house. Now go, if that's all right with you."

She stood and began to clear the table, taking the empty bottles and placing them in the sink before going to the fridge for fresh beer.

As the six of them stood to do her bidding she said, almost resignedly, "Tell Kennie to come and take Walter and Gracie for a swim until it's cooler. When they've done that I want the stables mucked out and they can feed the chooks. Tell Owen to collect the eggs, and I'll give him his reading after we've had dinner. All right, shoo!"

The two boys were outside under the lawn sprinkler waiting for them, and the message passed on one of them went back into the kitchen and reemerged with the littlies in tow. They stripped in the big conservatory and left their clothes over a chair before skipping out onto the lawn to jump laughing under the sprinkler.

Emma stood back a moment watching the newcomers intently, until nodding to herself she led the way across the lawn past an old house and before disappearing from view turned to beckon them.

Nicolas was reading her body language and turned to say, "Um, yes, Jennie gets cranky if we leave our clothes lying around so we better go up to Edoras first. We'll show you around. And, ah, as you can see, we sort of, get naked, and go around like that, when we're home anyway. It's a protest we make against the alienation of contemporary Western society, forgetting what it is to be a human being, sort of. That's what we say if anyone asks, but we like it anyway."

Peter and Alex glanced at each other, and after a moment shrugged and turned to follow.

Past the huge broken fig tree Alex caught up a little and said quietly, "Take it a bit easy, all right. We haven't got body issues, it's not like that. We've been living up in the desert, aside from going back down to Adelaide for school, but in the culture men and women don't do things together like this. We're recognised as young warriors and we don't bathe with the women and children, sounds a bit sexist maybe, but that's the way it is."

Nicolas looked at him oddly while Sarah stopped suddenly and lagged behind, looking away.

When they arrived up the hill at a big Medieval-looking hall straddling the ridge they went up the front steps and entered a huge open space with no rooms or partitions, on the left of which was a long wooden refectory table and on the right an enormous king-sized bed with extra sleeping pallets scattered about. Back of the long table was a big open kitchen dominated by a great old slow combustion stove overhung with drying herbs, and sausages and sides of bacon. Along the wall were kitchen cabinets stacked with dinnerware. Behind the big bed on the right hand side next to the kitchen was an oversized spa bath with a shower head and next to that a series of wardrobes and chests of draws, with a mirrored dressing table in the middle.

The theme was all cabinetry, carpentry, woodwork, almost as if it were a hobby of theirs, apart from the big iron stove and the kitchen tiling, the high roof supported by tall tree trunks and the floor clad in fine parquetry up to the kitchen and bath area which was intricately patterned with tiles, the motif continuing up the back wall behind the hanging herbs and smallgoods. Emma turned to greet their guests, smiling shyly in welcome, while they stood back gazing about in wonder.

Sarah didn't wait for their response but threw her shift and panties onto the bed and went back out to join the children down at the swimming hole. Robbie glanced after her, grinning quietly to himself.

Nicolas couldn't help himself. "We built all this, did you know? Wally helped us, before he died, and Chas, and we had a builder out from town to do the construction, but we did all the rest. And then Robbie went and did his apprenticeship with him, so he's a builder too now, and studying traditional architecture."

He stood back grinning like a little boy.

"And Em did all the tiling and parquetry."

As they gazed about Robbie stripped and folding his clothes neatly left them on the bed, then folded Sarah's and left them beside his before following her. At the door he turned to glance back a moment at their guests, then went back to the bed and bundled the folded clothing, tucking it under his arm, and disappeared out the door.

Emma watched him leave, frowning slightly. "I'm afraid you've offended Sair," she said quietly. "She considers herself a healer, and you've insulted her."

"Yes," Nicolas broke in, "and she's very good too, the best."

Alex cocked his head.

"If she wants to learn to be a healer, she can come with us back up into the desert next trip and I'll introduce her to some of the old ladies, maybe Peter's grandmother, and his uncle."

He stopped there, and went back to looking around the big house.

"Where do you work? I mean, where do you study, and do your writing?" he wanted to know suddenly.

"Oh, yes, downstairs under the front porch; that's my study, or else we use the school a lot, in the old house where Marcus and Liz live, and Karl shares. Do you want a look?"

Instead of replying Alex glanced at Peter, and turned, looking around, then went and pulled out a chair at the long table and sat down. Peter came over sat next to him.

Emma watched them a moment before going out through a back door in the corner next to the stove, and returned with two bottles of cold beer. Nicolas went around and took some clean glasses from one of the dining cabinets.

Alex waited while they did the honours before taking a sip, and nodded in approval.

He looked up.

"OK," he said, "you're nice people, pretty well adapted. I guess you know about me from all the papers, and I guess things have happened to you that I don't know about. After what they did to us Thursday I can imagine. But, shit, I don't even know what I'm doing here."

He leaned back, gazing about, and forward again. "What I mean is, and I don't want to be rude, we only came across here to enroll at Uni, because Sam was offered a job here, that's gone really sort, pear shaped, and now here we are, out here on this place talking to you. I don't even know who you are, or what all this is about, at all."

They stared at him, hurt and bewildered.

"Sorry, um, but we flew up to Alice Springs in January for a Big Meeting, that's what we've been doing, then we drove across from there to Northern NSW to stay on a cattle station for a few weeks. After that we went to Melbourne for a couple of days before flying over here. Sam went back to Adelaide to pack our things, and he was already here when we arrived. Next morning we went across to the university to enroll, where we ran into you guys. We went into town for a look-see, but got sodomised by a couple of cranky cops. Now we're here. Would someone like tell us, I mean, What the Fuck?"

Nicolas blinked. He turned to Emma and said, "Em, he doesn't know who we are, but we know who he is. Isn't that something? The real power of the media - panopticity - I must look into it. Remind me, will you, if I forget."

She reached over and took his hand, squeezing it and shaking her head.

"I'm sorry Alex, we don't know either, really," she said quietly. "Nic sort of relates to you, in a way, because he was arrested on a charge of carnal knowledge - it was with us, me and Sarah - when he was 13, but it was us not him. He was such a beautiful boy, still is, not just physically; he has the most beautiful mind and the most innocent heart. He was lucky because we had a really good sergeant in town who said it was all hearsay and not in the public interest to pursue, and a really good lawyer, so the whole thing was dropped. Then a few other things happened."

"When he read about you in the papers he realised there were other boys being targeted by those dreadful authority people, it wasn't just him, so in his mind you're larger than life. And now suddenly you're here, in our house, OK?"

Alex studied her face.

"OK, so what about you and Sarah, and Robbie?"

She chuckled at that, smiling, eyes bright. "For us? No, you're just so sexy, that's all. Peter is too, drop-dead spunks, both of you. You're seriously hot, and we're, sort of, liberated. After Nic was arrested, and all that other business, the four of us decided to be married, because we really love each other, and we built this big house so we can be together, up here away from the others. If we like a nice boy, that's OK too, except Robbie and Nic seem to be fairly satisfied and don't fool around much. It's mainly," she blushed, "helping some of the boys to grow up, if you know what I mean."

"Up here, in front of everyone?"

She looked puzzled for a moment. "Oh, no, it's not what you think. When Nic's working on his plays and his short stories he doesn't like to be disturbed - he sort of gets lost in it - but then he works all night and falls asleep so we built an extension downstairs, and anyway he has a swag next to his desk as well, because sometimes he'll just crash. It really worked out well; Sarah does her clothes and theatre costumes and sewing down there, and her healing - downstairs is our creative art space - because upstairs here is too busy and practical."

Alex and Peter exchanged glances, grinning, before Alex straightened his face again.

"All right, maybe not too bad an arrangement," he replied. "Sam never complained when we had our girlfriends over, in Adelaide. Now I understand what Jennie - she's your mother, isn't she - what she was annoyed about, a bit of decorum in public; is that right?"

Emma nodded, smiling. Nicolas sat there wide-eyed like a child, taking it all in.

Chapter Fifteen

The late afternoon was still hot, so after draining the two bottles of cold beer the four of them went down the ridge to the big swimming hole for a quick dip. The others we getting out when they arrived and Robbie and Sarah were pulling on their loose summer clothing while the kids played on the soft grass. When Alex stripped before diving into the water he gave Sarah a quick glance. She looked at him quizzically a moment before turning away to shepherd the children back up the long slope and over the ridge down toward the big house.

They bathed there quietly, thoughtfully, until Alex looked up and asked to be shown around the property.

Emma glanced at Nicolas and nodded, smiling, and they stepped up onto the grassy bank and giving themselves a quick rubdown with their clothes put them on. Peter and Alex did the same thing.

As they breasted the ridge they took in the panorama of the place, with its tiered amphitheatre planted with rows of late summer vegetables, and young olive trees laden with early fruit. At the bottom in front of a big outdoor stage was a cleared area planted to green freshly mown lawn like the swimming pool. Behind that were packing sheds, so they made their way down the path to take a look.

Nicolas was like a nervous little boy again, chattering excitedly about their plans and what they wanted to do next, but talking so fast he was difficult to follow. In a nutshell, their original idea for an annual folk festival had gone bad because of the drugs, and the expense and bad vibes generated by trying to police the event. So now it was more private and select; mostly older academics and intellectuals from Marcus's and Karl's old circle who came up from Perth every now and then, especially for their Easter break. The first big shed behind the stage closest to the two houses had been converted to an indoor auditorium, with lights and sound system installed. Here they took music students during the school week, after school. The next shed housed their tractors and farm machinery, while the third now housed stables at the back, and at the front a small nut nursery.

Peter and Alex stopped to admire the horses.

"Do you ride?" Nic wanted to know suddenly. "In the morning we can ride over to the new farm and I'll introduce you to my brother Eric, if he's back. He's a real cattleman now, we run Angus on the place. We buy our bulls from a stud over in NSW that's set up as a research station, with a school on it that's adjunct to Mount Tambla Grammar - we get some good ideas from them, you know."

Alex nodded, "Belkoomie. Yes, we know Mr Collins. It was his place we stayed at before we came over here, Eurongera Station."

Nicolas stopped, eyes popping, then started hopping about chuckling to himself like a demented elf. "Hear that, Em? Did you hear that? Magic! The world's full of magic! I told you so! Yes, I was right all along, I knew it. Always trust your instincts, isn't it!"

Emma glanced helplessly at the others, smiling, waiting until Nic settled again.

"Anyway," he said finally, "in the morning we'll go for a ride, all of us. Meet Chas too, that's Emma's Dad, the seriously best person. He runs the cattle side of things. And Auntie Elsie, she helps me with the nuts, and they're her sheep. She has a farm too, out the other side of town that we use to graze cattle and sheep, and goats - she's into goats now, Caprettos for the restaurant market."

He stood there a moment grinning from ear to ear, victorious.

"Now I'll show you my nuts." he stopped, giggling slightly. "Not my nuts, I mean, my nuts; my nut trees. We have pistachios, not too much trouble with them here unless we get rain over summer, but the rest are almonds, and walnuts and pecans. Emma pickles the walnuts, certified Organic, as well as her olives, and onions and cucumbers that we grow for her. All Organic, you know, we have all our certifications, finally, took a few years. They're very strict. We'll have the two other farms covered soon, so Elsie can have her Certified Organic Capretto. We'll do some for you one day, when you're out again, on a spit. You won't believe the flavour."

Exiting through the front of the last shed while he prattled on, Nic led them along the track bordering the two front paddocks planted to nut trees, all three to four years old, with a small mob of sheep grazing, and resting scattered about in the shade.

Alex stood there gazing about, shaking his head in wonder. "How do you find time to do all this?" he wanted to know.

They looked at him oddly.

"How can you not? We all help each other, it's one big family, and we work hard. That's the easy part, being productive. The problem we have is being able to sell it all. We need access to bigger markets, which means media and advertising. I've already said that, the whole thing is panoptic but for us we're on the wrong side of the mirror, if you know what I mean."

Strolling back toward the house Alex turned suddenly.

"OK, we're in. I'll get Auntie Edie to set up a business structure, maybe an agency. If you're using Belkoomie Angus bulls that helps a lot. We'll get you onto Landline, ABC, or SBS even, get a camera crew out here. They'll respect your privacy, we'll sort something out. We have to get your stuff into the big food warehouses; they can't waste shelf space so we have to get the demand sorted out first. But then again, maybe not, the boutique outlets might be better, and leading restaurants if we can get talking to the chefs. If we do it that way we can do our own deliveries. Sydney and Melbourne, and Perth, don't worry about Brisbane, they do the tropical thing."

He glanced at Nicolas, thinking, then added, "You're doing Anthropology and Literature, same as me, isn't it? Except I'm majoring in Media and you're more interested in Theatre. You should talk to Sam about Film. Might work, you know."

He walked off toward the big house at that, leaving Nic and Emma both standing there now grinning happily like small children whose Christmases had all come at once, while Peter looked on utterly bemused.

Back in the kitchen Alex stepped around the table behind Sarah, sitting there brushing her long hair after her swim, listening distractedly to the ongoing discussion among the adults. He paused and placed his hand lightly on her shoulder, and she reached up and squeezed it. When he sat down she cocked her head slightly in his direction.

After dinner as they made their way back up to Edoras she took his hand and led him into the studio under the front porch, while the others went up the steps into the hall.

Chapter Sixteen

There was no time next morning to go riding. They were all up at daybreak as turned out to be usual, and Sarah was making them a breakfast of flapjacks with fresh butter and honey while Emma sat practicing her flute, with a really nice Colombian Pitalito mountain coffee in the percolator. The lovely sound and delicious aroma wafted through the huge pillared living space under the tall roof, the early sun slanting through giving the place a soft glow, almost cathedral, with tiny dust motes floating about in the cool dawn air.

Alex sat there dreamily wondering, no matter where he found himself in Australia, wherever he happened to be, he was perpetually enchanted by the new day, as the birds started singing and the dawn broke, and everything came alive once more. Nobody spoke.

The mood was interrupted by Sam coming up the steps. He came in the front door and stood gazing about. They were all naked, hair tousled and bleary-eyed, except Sarah at the big stove who'd donned a full-length apron against spatterings from the frying pan.

"Want me to come back later?"

"What? No, you'll be right. Come in," Alex answered sleepily, distracted.

He stood and pulled on a pair of briefs. Peter did likewise, and almost as afterthought, as a courtesy to their visitor, so did Nicolas and Robbie. Emma simply went back to playing her flute, ignoring him so as to maintain her focus on the sheet music in front of her.

As Sarah brought over a great platter of flapjacks Robbie went around to the sideboard and set the table, before going across to the stove and bringing the percolator back placed it on a woven wooden mat on the table. They all sat and quietly started breakfast, none speaking until they'd had their fill and leaned back to enjoy the coffee.

"What's up, Sam?" Alex wanted to know finally.

"Thought I'd go into town with Bill, maybe stay with him a few days and have a look at all this shit going down. You can stay here if you want, or come with me and we can go back to Perth from there. Orientation Day won't be until next Friday, if you want to be there for that, so we can take our time."

Alex turned to the others. "When are you guys going back to Perth?" he asked. "Where are you staying, anyway, during semester?"

"Crawley," Robbie answered, "pretty much on the river. Marcus has an apartment there so we use that when we're in town. We all do."

Nicolas was watching them, and leaned forward suddenly. "You go with Sam," he said. "Go and see what's happening, you'll see, it's more important. I'll show you the other farm later, and you can meet Chas then, and Eric, if they're back yet. Doesn't matter, not so important, you go with Sam."

Alex glanced across at Sarah, then Emma, and they both nodded.

"OK," he agreed. "What about you, Pete? Coming with us, or want to stay here? Don't blame you if you do."

Peter flicked a quick glance at Emma and nodded, "Yeah, stay here eh? Get into too much trouble with you, eh?" He grinned.

But then Nicolas leaned forward again, face serious. "Yes, better he stay with us. It's not very pretty in town and he'll attract attention. They don't like coons; that's what they say, sorry to be rude. We tried to help some of the local people a while back and it caused a real shit fight, but then they got their cultural centre far enough away from town to stay out of sight."

They sat stunned, listening, until Alex turned to Sam in askance.

"That bad, is it?"

"Afraid so," the other replied; "worse than that. Still want to come?"

Alex nodded.

Chapter Seventeen

Bill's place was what they called a Group Settler house dating from the 1920s, when thousands of unemployed and impoverished workers from the old depleted industrial suburbs of England were brought out to Western Australia following the Great War, in the vain hope of opening up new farming areas on as old impoverished and depleted soil.

The scheme was a massive failure, Bill observed in telling the story, with a Royal Commission held in 1925 to enquire into the affair. The walk-off rate was almost 95%, with many committing suicide or being carried out strapped onto stretchers against self-harm, gone mad in the isolation of the tall forest. Only about 300 remained in the whole of the southwest, of over 6,000 families brought out by the post-war government.

The place was just out of town, separated from the first of the streets by a dry brown football oval, with player's change rooms and time keeper's box with its high scoreboard about a quarter the way around to the south. The big oval doubled as a showground early November every year, and away over the other side was a series of low pavilions leased at peppercorn rent from the shire by the local agricultural society, and beyond them across an access track the backyards of the first houses belonging to the town proper.

Backing the house on the one side and the football club on the other was dense bush of dry Marri and Jarrah woodland with its usual scattered Banksia and Sheoak, and understory of karri hazel, Hardenbergia thickets and tall dry clumping grass, through which the constant faint rush of a waterfall on the river behind could be heard. A tall steel Colorbond fence on the oval side gave them a modicum of privacy, but the rest was surrounded by bush which came almost to the back of the two sheds.

"No man's land," Bill said with a wry grin as they carried their things in from the truck, glancing across the oval. "Used to be our old farm, what there was of it, but fuck 'em. Now we keep it that way."

As he spoke a thin, wild-looking boy with long tangled hair, clad only in tattered shorts, came running out of the bush. He stopped short, staring at the two strangers before stepping onto the porch waiting for Bill to open the front door. As he did so the boy held onto his trousers and hid himself from view, peeking wide-eyed around Bill's legs at the others.

"Meet Daniel," Bill said, matter-of-factly. "He has a cubby over there in the bush for when I'm away. Won't stay in the house by himself, only comes in to get food and takes it back with him. Otherwise he traps rabbits, and snares parrots - funny little fella."

"His mother does heroin," he added quietly. "Got herself pregnant in an ashram in India before being deported during the AIDS panic, and this is the result."

Inside he led them to the middle bedroom where there were three single beds, before taking his own gear into the front bedroom. In the back converted bathroom he'd installed two sets of fixed bunks. Daniel went in there and climbed up onto one of the top bunks that was already made up, and busied himself with something under the pillow. Then he climbed down and coming back into the living room turned on the small TV before settling himself on the big couch against the other wall to watch cartoons.

The house itself was surprisingly well built with its typical front pitched roof and long side gable walls painted a soft cream, and dark green casement windows down their length each with its own hood. It was solidly built with good Jarrah stumps and flooring, and Bill had maintained it in sound condition since his parents and two maiden sisters died. It was basic as houses go; big bare rooms with enclosed veranda at the front and a new bullnose porch built around the double door as shelter from the weather. The wall between the kitchen and main living room had been knocked out and replaced by a single stained Jarrah lintel to support the roof, so that part of the place was roomy and accommodating.

At one end of the big verandah was a cluttered office lined with bookshelves, and a big desk with a computer in the middle, and a modem and printer. At the other end were two plain school desks in disarray. In one corner of the living room was another desk with a computer covered with kid's gaming stickers, and in the other a television set. The opposite wall was lined with a big old moth-eaten couch and a number of shabby mismatched armchairs that looked as if they'd been brought in from the town dump, or somebody's recycling shed.

The bathroom originally containing only a shower recess, toilet and wash basin had been gutted and converted into a bunkroom, making three bedrooms in all, and he had built a new bathhouse with the same layout out the back, except accommodating a huge iron claw-foot bath as well as the shower and toilet, and wash basin. It had a laundry to one side with a washing machine and trough in one corner and a fermenter bubbling with home brew in the other, the wall stacked with cleanskin bottles, and next to them a big chest freezer. A covered walkway connected it with the house.

Past the new bathhouse there were two sheds, in one of which he parked his Landcruiser and in the other he'd assembled a workshop, a patch of cut lawn with a clothes line separating the two.

Once Sam and Alex had stowed their gear they sat at the big dinner table in the kitchen. Bill went to the big fridge for cold beer, and taking some glasses from the kitchen cabinet sat down and filled them.

Alex took a sip and sat back.

"Good beer you've got in these parts, Bill, but hell, you people drink a lot of it."

"Ha, keeps us sane!" the old bloke retorted, almost into space, before sitting back fingering his glass; gazing thoughtfully at the amber liquid.

He looked up again. "This is not our stuff. The old people brought it with them, in the first ships, not us. It's a very traditional brew. We learned it from them, those of us who survived and were looked after, once the Royal Commission was done."

"Those older people back then came out with shipwrights, and wheelwrights and blacksmiths, and cooks and manservants and whole prefabricated houses would you believe. They brought everything with them, entire households. I reckon they were Hobbits, you know, that's what I think. The mistake they made was agreeing to transport convicts, who hated them, and then our lot trying to make up the resulting labour shortage, after the Great War, and then the Depression happened, and the Second War."

Alex leaned forward.

"Is that where Nicolas comes in, and Emma, and Jennie and those people?" he wanted to know. "And you're such friends with them, like, not as if you're too different. And your name is Hanna, a Scottish name not English working class. What is it to you, yourself I mean?"

Bill sat back while Sam watched, both looking at him with renewed interest.

They were interrupted by soft footsteps on the front porch, and a scratching at the door.

Nobody moved straight away so Alex got up and went to answer it. There was another boy there, staring up at him.

Before he could respond Bill was up and standing beside him.

"Hey, Josh, what's happening? Want to come in?"

The boy glanced up again at Alex and going around him went inside, into the living room. Bill knelt and taking his face in his hands asked him again what was happening.

The boy's face was impassive, taut, eyes wide.

"Did you run away?" Bill wanted to know.

Josh nodded slightly.

"How's your Mum?"

The boy looked up again, trembling.

Bill stood.

"OK, don't be scared," he said. "Want me to ring her, ask how she is? Want to stay here with us tonight? Daniel can lend you some pyjamas, and there's play clothes in the box. I'll ring and ask your Mum, OK?"

Josh nodded.

Bill went over to the phone and dialing a number waited a moment before speaking briefly.

He turned and nodded. "We'll drop you off at school in the morning, OK? Auntie Margie's at home with your mother and your sister's at the Dawson's. Mrs Dawson will come and get you after school tomorrow."

Daniel was up by then standing next to them, and the two boys hand in hand sat down again to watch the last of the late morning cartoons. Bill put the phone down.

He went across to the fridge and taking out extra food began to prepare the kitchen, preoccupied, busying himself with cold meat and salad for lunch.

Alex returned to the table and sipped his beer before glancing at Sam. The noise from the TV in the living room stopped as Daniel switched it off, cartoons over, and the two boys went past to the converted bunkroom. They came out again naked heading out to the bathhouse, before Bill called them back.

"Hey, boys, what did I tell you? A few manners, eh? We have visitors. If you want to go out for a shower at least wrap a towel around your bottom."

They came back in, stopping a moment to look curiously at Sam and Alex before heading back into the bunkroom to reemerge with towels around themselves.

A few moments later Daniel came back into the kitchen from outside without his towel, and stood naked again looking at them, without saying anything.

Bill turned from the stove shaking his head.

"Ah, sorry," he said. "He's scared of the hot tap, and Josh can't reach. Do you mind going with them, Alex, and adjust the shower? Don't make it hot, just warm enough. Stand there until it's right, and have Daniel check it himself before he gets under - so he learns, alright?"

Alex stood and drained his glass, then followed Daniel out. Josh was waiting for him, jumping up and down anxiously wanting to pee, so he nudged him over to the toilet bowl before turning to adjust the shower taps.

When the boys finished their shower they returned to their room to dry themselves and get dressed, coming out in clean but crumpled shorts and t-shirts. They sat either side of Alex at the table, leaning in close to him as Sam looked on, and Bill nodded thoughtfully to himself then turned and began attending to lunch.

Daniel got up again and went into the bunkroom for a brush, and sat again with his back to Alex wanting him to brush his hair, and tie it into a pony tail.

"What's going on with Josh's Mum?" Alex wanted to know as he started work. The other boy looked sharply up at him.

"Mulled out, as usual," Bill replied with a sigh. "Had a bad week apparently, so she bought a handful of cones and a few bottles of wine on Friday after work and has been out of it since. No food in the house."

He gave the boys a plate of sandwiches each before placing a large platter of cold sliced lamb and fresh garden salad with baby potatoes on the table, inviting his guests to help themselves.

"Don't worry; all the kids come here for is to seek permission," he went on. "They don't want to know anything so long as the world's OK, and they can be themselves. That's the trick, isn't it? They're stressed to the max by time they get here, and really only need to be brought back down to some sort of smiling infantile state, and a good breakfast there for them when they wake up, so they can start building their day. And you smile back and give them their cuddle on the way out, and have dinner ready for them when they get home from school, and a bath and bedtime story. Let them have control. That's no problem. Problem is the welfare fuckers coming around in the meantime, looking for someone to screw like I'm some sort of cheap whore who's gonna smile and cop it sweet."

He gazed out the window at the trees, then back again.

"That churchy crowd reckons this is women's work, looking after children, but they can piss off too. They have a support network for local kids who get into strife, but the boys who come here don't even have a childhood, they don't know what it means, and they don't fit in."

After a moment he glanced back sharply. "The bedtime story's the real trick, you know, after a good feed. A good fairy tale, a few hob-goblins, a handsome prince and fairy godmother, so they learn to externalise instead of bottling everything up, that's the way to do it. Before you know it they're grabbing the book off you wanting to read it themself."

The old man went to the fridge for fresh beer, chuckling softly, then turned and offered one all round.

"Those cunts out there," he said aloud once they'd settled down to lunch, reflectively, talking to the wall almost, "are seriously up 'emselves. They can get fucked."

Chapter Eighteen

Soon after lunch another two older boys arrived together on their bikes.

"Where have you been, Bill?" one of them demanded to know.

"Hey Sunny, Tim, what's up? Sorry, had to go to a meeting," he answered, unperturbed, looking up from doing the dishes. He turned, wiping his hands, leaving Daniel to finish the drying up.

"Sean Miller shot himself, yesterday. The cops had him at the station giving him a grilling, and he went home and took his Dad's rifle, and shot himself."

"Oh, damn. Fuck it!" Bill looked away out the window a moment, shaking his head, then sighed and nodded briefly to himself.

"How's the family taking it?"

"Bit of a punch-up," the other boy Timmy interjected, belligerent. "His father reckons he was a gutless little shit, should have spoken to him first, and he would've fixed it with the cops; didn't have to kill himself. His brother and sister are really cranky with the old bloke, reckon he caused it as much as the police, so there was a big screaming argument. His Mum's, sort of like, out of it, won't talk to anyone."

"OK," Bill nodded. "Who's the other boy got arrested? What's he in for?"

"Jordie? No, he didn't do anything. He was going steady with Ellie Connolly, and her father gave her a hiding and grounded her, then had the cops arrest her boyfriend. He went into her room and stole her diary, that's how he found out. That's not fair."

The old man watched their faces, frowning. "But she's only twelve, and he's fifteen, what did you expect."

The boys looked genuinely confused.

"Well, just turned fifteen and she's nearly thirteen," Sunny explained. "They were steady. They got together at the school dance; everyone knew they were going out. Her Dad's a cunt anyway, a mad bastard. Who else does she have to look after her, her stupid mother?"

"Anyway," Tim broke in, "it's not like she'd just turned twelve and he was nearly sixteen, is it? That'd be a bit rank. It's not like that, they were going out steady. Everyone does."

Bill sat at the table, then turned and sent the littlies outside to play.

"Welcome to Barkhan Crossing," he muttered wearily.

He turned back again to the two older boys. "All right, there's a bit of cold lunch left if you're hungry; make yourselves some sandwiches," he said. "Staying here tonight, or what are you up to?"

"Ah, can we stay here, maybe a few days?" Sunny asked, nervously shifting from one foot to the other.

"Sure, of course you can, you know that. And thanks for asking. What's on at your place? Who are you living with at the moment, Brigit or Pedro?"

"Yeah, Mum, but if you ring Pedro it'll be OK with him. She's not making any sense, had a hell party Friday night. Daren and Sky brought a big shitload of coke and eckies down from Perth. Somebody else got hold of ice from somewhere, and it just went wild, fuckin', like, crazy. I got out of there, staying at Timmy's place. His Dad knows we're here, we asked him if we could and he said yes if it's all right with you. He'll give you some money during the week."

Bill nodded, glancing across at Sam and Alex who sat there silently taking it all in.

"I suppose our friends Peters and Marchant were there, as usual?"

Sunny nodded, but then quickly turned to leave. "My stuff's at Timmy's place, can I go and get it? His stuff too. We'll need our school uniforms, and we haven't done our homework yet. If we don't do it we'll be in strife."

The old man simply waved them off and turned to finish the dishes. As they left he turned and called his shoulder, "In the morning take Daniel and Josh to school. Make sure they're properly dressed in their uniforms. After school, wait for Daniel and see he comes home with you. Josh is being picked up by Mrs Dawson, got it?"

"Yeah, no worries."

Sam leaned forward, real concern on his face.

"How on earth can you stand it, Bill? How do you afford it, must be costing you a fortune."

The other bent down and tapped his lower right leg with a spoon he had in his hand, making a hollow wooden sound under his long trousers.

"TPI, Vietnam," he said quietly. "Land mine, along with a bit of traumatic stress disorder. But I'm over that now, off medication since I got my degree and I started looking after the boys. I have a double degree actually, in Psych and Anthropology; took me a few years keeping the heebie-jeebies at bay, then wrote my Honours thesis on coming-of-age. Anyway, I got over it, and the boys keep me going. Best intelligence network you could imagine. Nothing happens in this town without one of them coming to tell me."

"And it's not as expensive as you think," he added, looking up. "I get meat from Nic's Auntie Elsie - we have a killing day now and then, and divvy it up. Jennie brings me fresh veges once or twice a week, depending on how many mouths to feed, so we do all right. Groceries are the big thing, but we get old stock past its use-by date. We get rolled oats bulk, and honey in bulk too from the bee keeper who works the Tuart forest a bit north of here, and milk. And as you see, the parents chip in occasionally."

He waved the spoon casually around the house. "I own the place, freehold, got no debts and can't complain. One fine day I'll drop off the perch, I guess, and hope someone else will take over, or better we've got the town sorted out by then. I'm not holding my breath. Nicolas is the primary beneficiary of my will, you see, so their family will probably run things. He's a certified bloody genius, that boy, astonishing, and has a heart of gold after all he's been through."

"Anyway, now you know. It's not just here, every bloody where, the state's run by cowboys and branch managers, think they know shit, but all they do is waste time and money covering their own arse. The place is far too isolated. Nobody is answerable to anyone, they have no clear thinking and no discipline, and nobody else gives a crap."

"There's too much loose mining money in the economy, like too much blood sugar in your system; too much caffeine. If we let these boys go they'd be picked up by Welfare and put in some hostel up in Perth, where they'll be on drugs with the rest of them, and after that a spell or two in jail trying to cool them off. Their lives are fucked by then."

"The way it is now, our boys are getting into University, or WAAPA, or doing a trade. We make them earn their keep," he went on. "Nic's older brother Grant did an apprenticeship with their father up at Wallaga, after their mother suicided, and Chas took in Eric after Frank and Simon were killed, and taught him to ride and wear decent clothes, and made a good man of him. He was a serious risk, that boy, a real worry, but when you meet him you'll be surprised what a fine young fella he turned out to be."

He looked up from his soliloquy, shaking his head with a wry grimace. "Wonder any of us is still sane, wouldn't you?"

He paused a moment watching through the window at the boys playing outside. They had their clothes off again and were gamboling about under the sprinkler. He went out taking their towels out to them, and brought their shorts and t-shirts inside.

By the time he was back in the kitchen and at the table Alex and Sam were in conversation.

"That's it, isn't it?" Alex was saying. "We can do it. Just keep doing that other job the way they want, and keep your eyes peeled for a few clues, and we can be making this film as well, like that ex-boxer Tiger

Monk bloke with those street kids up in the mountains in Thailand. We can have it both ways, and they won't even know about it until we've done our Melbourne or Sydney release, maybe the Sydney Film festival."

He turned to Bill. "How famous do you want to be?"

Bill snorted, and chuckled, shaking his head. "Leave me out of it, mate, that's my advice."

Chapter Nineteen

Alex and Sam returned to Perth on Tuesday and started going over some preliminary scripts based on the Law brief, seeking to cover lost ground and provide a more accurate reflection on the reality they'd experienced in place of the hype, dry argument and distracting imagery of the original project - trying to persuade some judge, or Law students somewhere, of something. For two long days they sat going over old footage, covering the work they'd done up in the Central Desert, and in Adelaide. There was nothing they'd done in the past that had quite prepared them for the raw, deeply embedded power play; the subtlety, intricacy, and underlying brutality of the situation here.

Peter arrived late Thursday morning just before lunch with a broad grin and Emma in tow. Sarah followed them in with Robbie and Nicolas and stood gazing about.

"Not too crowded," she said off-handedly. "Maybe we should rearrange things a bit, make one place out of the two and share things around. We're only three blocks away; it'll be good."

She paused, thinking. "I know some girls with a flat near here; we can make a sort of distributed urban commune and go to the city markets and buy bulk. They'll like you boys."

Sam turned to her, frowning, which was perhaps a mistake because he didn't get a word in.

"Sam, what about you?" she wanted to know, rotating in his direction. "I mean, you're an old guy but you must have somebody? Is there somebody? I'm curious."

Alex sat back, grinning. "Denise. That's his fiancée - school teacher out at Warmunya. Well, she's headmaster now, actually - they're both too busy - and she doesn't get it."

Peter giggled, embarrassed, causing Alex to add, "Well, because we are brothers, Sam and us, tribally you know, she's our wife too. No idea. The old ladies worry about her and try to find her another brother to us, to keep her happy while Sam's away, but she just doesn't get it."

Sam stood abruptly and went to the kitchenette, bustling about with lunch.

Sarah followed him. "Sorry, Sam, just having fun; I didn't mean anything. It's your business, right?"

Alex followed her and took her arm, glancing at Sam who glanced back, annoyed.

"They're getting married next Christmas, supposedly after this film contract is done. But he's good, eh? Never complains about me or Peter, only makes sure we use condoms, and don't get into strife. He's helped us a lot with our homework and we both got really high marks. He and Nic need to work together more, and Bill, you know. It's important. This new film we're going to do is important."

"Our room'll still be free," he paused, adding as an afterthought.

"Let me have that bigger room then," Sam interrupted from the breakfast bar. "Allow me a bit of space. And if you guys want to fool around here it's one at a time, and weekends, right? I have serious work to do."

Emma nodded. "Yes, we'll do the shopping then, Saturday mornings. Anything in the meantime I'll come over and see what you need. This place can be a study area, like Karl's house."

They all looked at one another, agreeing. Nicolas hadn't said anything but stood back, smiling in his odd, oblique way.

Robbie stepped forward to fill the new gap and said, "Sair, who are these other two chicks? You hadn't mentioned them."

Alex looked up in protest. "Yeah, what's going on? We'll go and see them eh? They'll be home, do you think?"

Sarah grinned, teasing him, and Alex glanced over at Sam plainly wanting to be excused after two days of solid concentration.

Sarah took him by the hand anyway and started leading him out, Robbie coming in behind, while Nicolas simply shrugged on their way past, and then nodded, turning his attention to Sam.

"Just thinking about your film, Sam, what I can see of it, you and Alex. I wrote this play once," Nicolas was already saying, Emma watching him with a sudden interest, "an interpretation of Euripides. But nobody let me do it."

He turned to face Emma, palms out, holding her away, pacifying her before continuing.

"Well," he went on, "the thing was really only about shifting his *Bacchae* away from its tragic interpretation to reveal an underlying truthfulness on the human condition that's not necessarily tragic as such, rather illuminating, enlightening I thought, except nobody got it. I thought it'd become, like, repetitive, sort of, losing its power to articulate, anything. So I've been thinking a lot about it, you know, audience perception and context and pretext, all that stuff; it's intricate - today's world is awfully mixed up - but we do need to get a conversation happening."

He looked up, embarrassed, awkward. "Um, yes, sorry I talk a lot. I didn't mean to intrude. I've been working a lot with Marcus, he's a professor, and you have your doctorate already, but I'm just a kid yet, really. Can I show you what I've been doing?"

Peter watched him bright-eyed, intrigued, a smile beginning to show.

When Alex arrived back next morning with Robbie and Sarah, and Bec and Erin, he and Emma were in the double bed in Sam's room, Sam was stretched out in his bed, and Nicolas was sitting at the editing desk with his head down, keyboard aside, sound asleep.

Emma came out, disturbed by the chatter, and seeing him there motioned the two boys to help her get him undressed and into Alex's bed, leaving him lost to the world with only a single sheet on top against the hot day. She left the fan on and roused Peter and they showered and dressed, and had breakfast before rounding up the others to go see what Orientation Day had to offer.

Chapter Twenty

All next week they stood in long queues sorting out their lecture and tutorial timetables, at times separated into their various discipline streams and at others coming back together, before going off again to their first introductory lectures. Nicolas and Alex spent most time together having enrolled in the same subjects and found themselves in the same classes, and as they stood around waiting in line talked quietly about Sam's new film.

Nicolas' script was excellent. Alex listened to him with new respect, even though at times he had to pull him up while he talked on an on. He learned to be patient with him, slowly beginning to appreciate what he'd suffered through childhood and the high regard in which he was held by those who knew him, and the difficulty those who didn't had to face trying to make sense of what he was saying, and in that the nature of his disability. Being so very handsome didn't help much as he caught people's eye the moment he entered a room, yet at the same time confused them with his long complex sentences and the sophisticated ideas he sought to express.

It wasn't until Nicolas started telling him about inheriting the farm from old Wally Cavanaugh, Jennie's father and Emma's grandfather, before he was killed by the lightning strike that split the big fig tree near the old house, that Alex's ears really started pricking up. What he'd worked out with Chas and their lawyer was to set up a holding company and a number of subsidiary farming companies to underwrite their various operations, and make sure everyone was included in a way that inspired them and had them working together as one family, just as Alex had done with the gold mine at Anamenatjere in the Northern Territory. Aside from his obvious gifts, Nicolas was a corporate genius.

As the week rolled on Peter spent more time with Emma over at Marcus's apartment on the river, while Robbie more or less moved in with Erin and Bec. Nicolas started sleeping with Alex at Sam's place, heads constantly together, except when Sarah complained and Alex had to go stay with her occasionally while Bec wanted to visit Nicolas. She was already in second year Arts/ Law with a young brother Julian just starting first year, who'd joined the campus Labor Club before even enrolling. When he came over for dinner Friday night to meet everyone he prattled endlessly about Capitalism and the Illuminati, and the growing peril of Neoliberalism in global affairs. Toward the end of their meal he stopped suddenly, realised nobody was listening, became agitated, and getting up from the table left abruptly.

Next week came and went as lectures got underway, and tutors patiently sorted their classes into working groups, handing out course outlines and reading lists. They lined up again at the campus bookshop to get their unit readers, and bagfuls of books. The place was entirely linear, to catch Nic's turn of phrase, and he was right; 15,000 students queued up in long lines one after another, to be processed over the next three years and more into their various discipline majors to emerge in the fullness of time recognised as knowing something, as being somebody, except that was all a long way off yet.

Right now they were nobodies, they quickly realised, stripped entirely of identity and assigned numbers before being herded around; the inviting architecture and beautiful gardens vanishing rapidly into the subliminal in favour of endlessly long bare corridors trying to locate remote, out of the way tutorial rooms, and arrive breathlessly late.

Their initially exuberant social life as rapidly deteriorated. Sam sat back watching, occasionally nodding and smiling to himself, and said nothing. When Marcus arrived later that week to see how they were all going he did likewise.

As Easter approached Marcus refused to allow Nicolas to take time out from his study to help prepare their annual music fest. There was a big argument about it and Nic went for long walks by himself, finally mollified by the Undergraduate Dramatic Society agreeing to do Howard Barker's *The Fence in Its Thousandth Year* fresh from the Perth Festival, and be paid for their performance. He was still shy with them, uncertain how to proceed, and anyway his first year units contained no theatre which was upper level study unavailable until next year.

Finally he decided to stay with Bill Hanna over the long weekend. He wasn't sulking, he tried to explain, only realising that he'd been running the Easter festival for five years and made a lot of money out of it - all the way through his adolescence - but now things were changing in his life. And he had a new friend, he added, glancing quickly in Alex's direction, and residual issues he wanted to address.

Alex nodded, reassuring him. He in turn had to mollify Sarah, saying it wasn't sexist but Bill's was a place for troubled boys. As she voiced her protest Nicolas stepped forward to take her by the hand, then held her, talking softly in her ear, and she relaxed.

Sam decided to film the festival and stay on the farm with Marcus, with Peter as his assistant.

Emma went with Peter.

Chapter Twenty One

There was only the one early lecture on the Thursday before Good Friday and they were home by ten thirty, packed and ready to leave by twelve. After a quick lunch Marcus took Robbie and Sarah with him in his Volvo. Sam followed with Peter and Emma in the Landcruiser, while a bit later when they were ready Nicolas left with Alex in Wally's old Bedford farm truck that he still liked to drive.

By time they arrived at the farm the other cars were parked in the shed with nobody to be seen. They must be in the big house. Nicolas pulled up under the old split fig tree and got out, going around the back to get their bags.

Eric came out of the far end shed in his plaid jackeroo shirt, moleskins and riding boots to see who it was, and when he saw Nic strode down along the driveway to greet him. The two brothers said nothing, merely shook hands and embraced, then turned to greet their guest.

Alex could see their resemblance, and there in his own moleskins and boots made an immediate impression. Straight away, however, he saw how opposite they were; Nicolas animated, nervous, garrulous, and Eric reserved and watchful. It wasn't simply the difference in age; Eric barely fifteen with still soft post-pubescent skin and bum fluff on his top lip while Nic had already learned off with sharper pre-adult features and clear shadow for want of a shave. He thought how well Eric might fit in up at Eurongera with the MacFarlane boys, and made a note of it.

Eric anyway shook hands warmly, with a strong grip, and telling Nic to leave their stuff led the way back up to the last shed where Chas was inspecting a horses' offside front hoof. He eased it down and straightened up as the boys strode in, stepping forward to offer his hand in greeting. Formalities out of the way he turned back to the horse, worrying over its infected hoof before asking Nicolas over to look at it.

Eventually they turned and came over to where Eric had Alex sitting on a bare wooden bench, sipping a cup of tea.

"How long have you been back?" Alex asked, for want of conversation. "I thought we'd just missed you by a day or two, when we were here in February."

"Ah well, you know the way it is," Chas said taking his cue, watchful like Eric. "Bit of trouble with our pasture, being so dry this year, but we'll be right. How're yer goin' yourself, eh? Heard a bit about you son, making a go of it, eh? Got yourself into university with Nicolas I hear."

Alex sat back, ball in his court, vast differences between the overlapping worlds he inhabited at such a young age flooding his thoughts - aside from Sam and Peter being his only close family - treading carefully in each of them. He leaned forward, frowning, and sat back again to sip his tea; after two months on campus trying to think about offering some logical analysis, or merely reverting back to his own self.

"Well, sorry about your music festival," he leaned forward again and said finally, earnestly. "I'm just going on a sort of gut feeling, but Nic and I, he said anyway, will be camping at Bill Hanna's place over the weekend. There's some other stuff we want to be looking at, about your boys here in town. We have the same trouble up there at Warmunya, like. We have a sacred place way out at Puntayeri where the men and boys go, away over the Territory border from here, and odd bits of money coming in now from our mine on the Queensland side, but it's still not easy."

Chas stood, eyeing him, then went back to worrying over the horse's hoof, and picking her leg up cleaned out what was left of the dirt. Deciding it was nothing serious he drenched it clean and applied a poultice before setting it down, observing the way she kept her weight off it. Backing her gently out of the stall he let her go out the back onto the clean grass of the amphitheatre, and shut the gate.

After she'd gone he turned to exit through the big front door of the shed. "Yeah, no worries," he said quietly on the way out. "You're good lads, do what you need to do."

They watched him go. The three of them sat back finishing their tea before Eric leaned forward and tapping Nicolas on the knee stood to leave. Nicolas glanced at Alex and nodded.

"Um, yeah, doesn't happen much, eh," Eric began as they went outside. "We don't shoe our horses - causes more harm than good. Fluffy went off the other day and stepped in some old barbed wire up there on the reserve I reckon, with those fetlock scratches. Came home this morning bobbing a bit so thought we'd better have a look at her. She'll be right, eh?"

Alex glanced sideways at him, acknowledging the overture. The brothers while the resemblance was there were two different kittles of fish. Unlike Nicolas Eric was street smart, by the way his eyes constantly darted about taking in every detail, with his wry grin and disarming manner; not so cunning as sharp and constantly alert. Eric was flash, too, his cowboy outfit neatly pressed and boots polished, with his Akubra set back on his head more like a Country and Western singer than a working jackeroo.

"I wouldn't know," he answered finally, "not that good with horses. We did a lot of riding up at Eurongera over the holidays but I haven't really started learning anything yet. You'd be telling me, I reckon."

The other nodded, face open suddenly and a shy fleeting smile at the compliment that he quickly hid again from view, making Alex think of Little Artie, and far more to him than met the eye. But why the composed features and darting eyes? They walked on.

As they approached the old house Eric asked Nicolas suddenly, frowning and without looking at him. "Who's at Bill's?"

"Daniel. Sunny and Tim, I bet . . . . Depends, maybe Lou and Alan."

"Alan topped himself, hanged himself, eh. Cops were chasin' 'im. About three weeks ago. Lou might be there, yeah, prob'ly."

Alex stopped, stunned, but the brothers walked on regardless. Past the last shed Eric turned to gaze after him.

"Ah, what we might do is bring 'em out to the farm, eh?" he called back. "That'd be better than staying in town, this weekend anyway. Bill'll be happy, place'll be hell. They can ride their bikes over here on Saturday for the music; Chas an' me'll be doing a bit of Country, and maybe some Bluegrass. The jazz bit in the afternoon, that's Karl's thing, so they'll prob'ly want to go for a swim after we've finished. The evening show, after dinner, Liz an' Emma want to do some flute stuff, but they've got this new play on as well."

Nicolas stood rubbing his jaw, thinking, his mind elsewhere. "We might go now," he said after a pause, "before the traffic, and Clint Marchant starts his shift. Cunt he is. We'll take Sam's truck, the Landcruiser, they'll want to bring their bikes."

Chapter Twenty Two

Bill was glad to see them when they arrived. Daniel was hanging onto him, not wanting him to go, not quite understanding that Bill wanted him to go stay on the farm with the other boys over Easter so he could take a break.

Eric was right. As Sunny and Tim who were already there quickly loaded their bikes in top of the truck another boy Lou arrived, who after a quick look around picked his bike up and put it up on top with the others then threw his backpack on the back seat.

Nicolas stepped up onto the porch, apologetic that he hadn't phoned. Still looking at Bill he ruffled Daniel's long unkempt hair and drew him close, then went inside. Daniel simply turned and followed, finger in his mouth. Alex watched the way Nicolas had with the boy, and strode up the steps after him.

Bill stood there patiently as they all trooped in and out, until they settled and took drinks from the fridge, and clean glasses from the kitchenette, and sat around the table helping themselves. He sat on the top step, leaning against the veranda post gazing out across the oval until finally Sunny came back out and asked what he was doing. He sent him off with a length of rope to secure their pushbikes.

Daniel came out and Bill took him into his lap, speaking quietly to him. When Alex came to see what they were doing Daniel got up and took his hand, and leading him to the truck opened the front door and got in. Bill stood and came over, saying through the window that he'd be out in the morning, alright?

As Alex started driving out a pale blue Volvo was coming around the oval toward them, kicking up a trail of dust in its wake. Sunny leaned forward to tap him on the shoulder to stop.

"That'll be Pedro," he said, and Nic stopped to wait for him.

As the Volvo pulled up alongside a lean, rangy, weather-beaten bloke with the huge forearms, splayed hands and flat fingers of a bricklayer got out and stepping over to the truck inspected each of the occupants in turn. His gaze settled steadily on Alex.

"Who's 'e?" he wanted to know.

"Ah, mate from Uni," Nic replied. He turned his head to introduce them. "Alex, that's Pedro, Sunny's Dad . . . . . Pedro, Alex Lennox, from Adelaide."

Pedro continued to stare at him, until tossing his head slightly in dawning recognition he said, "Ah yeah, you're that coon's mate, coupla months ago, the boys roughed up. Gotcha."

Alex sank back into his seat.

"Well, yeah, that was Daren and Sky and their mates. Gave 'em a bit of a speakin' to, eh. Do it again I'll rip their fuckin' balls off. Fuckin' knob 'eads, the lot of 'em. Towns full of 'em."

"Have any more trouble give us a hoy, right?" he added after a pause. "How is 'e anyway, all right? No 'ard feelin's?"

"No, he's good, didn't say anything about it; doesn't want any trouble." Alex leaned forward again slightly. "Better tell them not to fuck with him, though. He's from a real big traditional community up in the Territory. If he decided to do anything they'd get a spear in their leg, like, payback you know. He'd do it himself, wait his chance, he'll be right."

Pedro glanced up sharply, and suddenly began a jig there on the spot, chuckling to himself. "Ha, bloody bewdy, fuckin' way to go! Tell 'im to do Marchant while 'e's at it, fuckin' needs it that cunt."

He stopped suddenly, abruptly turning his attention to Sunny sitting there in the back with Kim and Lou. "How yer going, Sunny? What are you up to?"

"Ah, not staying at Bill's," Sunny said quietly. "Staying at Chas's place with Eric. Taking our bikes, but we can ride the horses if we want, and go swimming, that's about it. Maybe go to the concert on Saturday."

"Yeah, all right, no worries." he reached around to his back pocket and took out a thick battered leather wallet, removing a handful of big notes. "Here's some money, all right. I'll give it to Nic for your keep."

"Give 'em fifty bucks if they need it," he said to Nicolas. "Might come out meself Sat'day, be good. But you better piss off, eh? Get clear of town before the rest 'o the knob-heads rock up. I just wanted to see how you were goin', thought I might run into ya on the off-chance, but I need to see Bill and I'll catcha later. If I don't see ya I'll catcha Monday or Tuesday."

Nic tucked the wad of notes into his shirt pocket and putting the truck back into gear released the clutch and drove off. Pedro left the Volvo where it was and walked the rest of the way to Bill's house, where Bill sat where he was leaning against the porch post waiting for him.

Chapter Twenty Three

"Pedro, what's up?" the old bloke wanted to know.

"Fuckin' storm brewin', mate. Aedan Donovan's rocked up, with Stookie, stayin' at Brigit's."

Bill nodded, rubbing his whiskers, and gazed across the oval toward town. "How far do you reckon we ought to let them go?"

"Dunno, fuck, could be anything. Sky's been getting his shit off 'im, prob'ly owes 'im. Aedan's come to collect I reckon. But he'll have to get 'round Peters first, they're the ones ripping Sky off, taking 'im down, him an' Marchant."

"What's Brigit got to do with it, your ex? What's it got to do with you?"

Pedro glanced sharply at him. "She's fucking Stookie. He's Amelia's father, you'd reckon she'd learn better by now, but tryin' to keep him happy, protect Sky. That's my opinion."

Bill rose slowly, favouring his gammy leg. "We'll get Mick over, eh? Bit of insurance."

He looked back over his shoulder as he went back into the house. "What's your other opinion?" he wanted to know.

"We're fucked. The old system was better. Yeah, get Mick over, and we can get Nic back later to explain it, the way he does, but, yeah." Pedro turned away, pacing back and forth, worrying.

Twenty minutes later an ancient Ford Falcon came around the oval, past the Volvo parked there in the dry grass, and pulled up next to the front porch. A big old bloke stooped as he got out, and glancing sideways at Pedro stepped up onto the porch and went inside.

A few minutes later he and Bill reemerged with a couple of cold bottles and clean glasses, and sat down again on the step. He called Pedro over.

"What's up, Pete? Come up and have a yarn, eh? Wanna beer?"

"Nah, it's right, Mick. Fuckin' hard cunt you are. But yeah, OK, no worries, eh?"

Mick calming him poured a cold beer and sat back. "Be like Australia Day, I reckon."

During the afternoon Bill came and went, bringing them fresh beer and occasionally something to eat. About six o'clock he went inside again for a while, coming out with a big wok full of pork stir-fried vegetables, with chopsticks for Mick and himself, and a fork for Pete.

They ate, and sat back waiting, Bill getting up again occasionally for beer, until precisely at eight a huge explosion rent the air and a great cloud of smoke rose, from their perspective right in the middle of town.

Pedro jumped and started running toward the Volvo, then stopped. Bill and Mick were still there on the porch watching him.

"Take it easy, mate," Mick said. "We'll be right." Bill went inside for a fresh bottle.

A little under an hour later a teenager about Nic's age came running breathless from the bush on the other side of the house, pulling up suddenly to see his father there.

Chapter Twenty Four

Bill with his gammy leg sat back in his chair at the kitchen table while big Mick leaned forward, Sky on the other side finishing the last of the stir-fry, scraping it up from the bottom of the wok with a fork before taking a spoon for the juice. Pedro by this time had turned on the TV set and was watching it from the old lounge in the living room.

"They took Daren," Sky said eventually. "Dumb cunt he is, anyway."

"What makes you different?"

"I'm here, eh?"

He looked up, grinning. "Fuckin' Peters, and Marchant, eh, should've seen 'em go up, minced fuckin' barbeque, straight to hell. Car's shrapnel, shit, all over the fuckin' street; shop windows on both sides out."

The two old boys sat back watching him.

Finally Bill stood and taking the wok to the sink gave it a good scrub and rinse, leaving it upside down on the dish rack to dry. He turned, wiping his hands on a tea towel before leaning forward to wipe the table with it.

He brushed close to Sky, then stood looking down at him.

"What brings you here then?"

"Ah, nothin'. Might be a bed. Stook's givin' me the shits, just wants to fuck Brigit, and see and that Aedan Donovan's a real arse 'ole, eh? No sense a humour. What the fuck."

"She's your mother, Sky," Bill sat back watching his face.

"Yeah, well, shit happens," after a moment. "Stay here's all right, is it? Got a towel?"

He stood and went into the bunkroom, and came back out shrugging, enquiring. Bill leaned back pointing to a back cupboard. Sky undressed and threw his clothes on the bottom bunk beneath Daniel's, and wrapping the towel around his middle went outside to the bathhouse.

Nobody said anything. Bill went over to get a cribbage board off the top of the fridge and set it down between him and Mick, and started to deal cards.

Half an hour later another big car rolled quietly to a stop outside but nobody stood to go see who it was. Sky by this time was pacing nervously back and forth, while Pedro had fallen asleep on the couch. Bill and Mick were still at the kitchen table playing crib.

"You fuckin' coming out Sky, or we have to come in and get you?" a gruff voice called from the front of the house.

Sky sat down at the table, trembling and not looking at anyone.

Mick watched him a moment, then slowly rose and went out the front door to stand on the porch, peering into the late evening gloom just beyond the light from the house.

"Got a problem, have you?"

"Hey, Mick," the voice answered. "Nah, no problem, just need to talk to Sky is all, about a few quid he owes."

The big man cocked his head. "Should've thought about that before you blew Peters up, and his offsider - they'd have it, I reckon. No good chasing the bloody kids around town. Waste of time, wouldn't you say?"

Another voice answered, "Ah, bullshit, we didn't do that. He there or not, cunt? I haven't got time for this crap."

The voice stepped forward to reveal a dapper, neatly dressed man holding a short rifle.

By this time Bill had come out onto the porch.

"Mr Donovan," he said. "You know the rules. We have an agreement, all of us. This is neutral ground, safe house for the kids, it's off limits."

"Ah, Hanna, fuckin' smart-arse cunt, I'll fuckin' shoot you first if need be. Just get that slippery little shit out here, eh, and we'll go about our business. No reason for you to get involved."

Bill didn't reply. He stood there holding his ground. Mick leaned forward slightly but Bill took his arm and held him steady. The first voice came forward into the light.

"Better do as he says, boys." It was Brian Stookie.

The two on the porch stepped forward and stood there, blocking the way. Donovan raised the rifle ready to shoot, but at that moment a long barbed spear whistled through the open corner of the porch from the bush beyond, striking him square in the chest. He staggered back and his shot went into the ground, raising a puff of dust. The rifle slipped from his fingers and he clutched in amazement at the shaft protruding from his chest. He adjusted his shirt front and his lapels, and reached around with his left hand tugging at the bloody point sticking out his back, preoccupied entirely with the thing - annoyed with it as if his nice suit was ruined. He sagged then dropped to his knees, head forward and jaw dropping, and fell sideways. His foot twitched a moment, then his bowel opened and stink filled the air.

Nobody said anything for a long tense moment, until Bill nodded finally and said quietly, "You might want to pick him up and take him to hospital, Brian. He mightn't be dead yet, eh, except he looks like he might be. Not moving any more, from what I can see from up here. If he is you might just put him in the boot and clear off."

"If you want to get the spear out," he added almost as afterthought, "push it through a bit and break the point off. Then you'll be able to pull the shaft out. You mightn't get him into the boot otherwise. Leave it there if you want, the boys'll clean up."

He nudged Mick and the two turned and went back inside. Pedro was on the couch no longer asleep, but sat there eyes wide, a wet stain at the front of his pants where he'd pissed himself.

Sky was lying on his back on the living room floor, pale and in shock, jeans down around his knees and bleeding heavily from a spear wound to his right thigh.

Bill nodded thoughtfully, gazing down at him. "Hhhmm, well, that's not something I'd wish on anyone," he muttered, "but there you go. Shit happens, eh?"

The big car outside started and drove off. He turned to Pedro. "Better take him to hospital, Pedro. Reckon you can manage? You'll be safe enough now, nobody'll trouble you."

He knelt down and pulled Sky's jeans right off and set them aside, rolling them carefully so the bloodstains were on the inside. His thigh while bloody and bruised was nonetheless clean, the entry wound sharp and clear. He took a bowl of warm water and added disinfectant, and knelt again to bathe it. He went out to the bathhouse a moment and quickly returning broke open some sterile packets and placed new pads on the deep cut before wrapping his thigh in clean gauze bandage.

"Want a hand?" he asked Pedro, and the other nodded, dumbly, without moving.

"Go and bring the car up close then, fuck ya - do something useful for a change."

Pedro looked up suddenly and stood to go. As he left the two old boys bent down and got Sky to his feet. He buckled under the weight but they held him up. He was still pale and shaking, small beads of sweat knitting his brow. They got him to the door and out onto the porch where Pedro had brought the Volvo up close to the steps, then opened the front passenger door and eased him onto the seat.

Bill shut the door and peered in through the window. "Right, all done. They weren't here, Pedro, none of this happened. You came over this arvo looking for the kids and you found them, then came up to the house for a beer. Mick came over to play crib and have a beer with his old mate, while the kids went out to Chas Larkin's for the weekend. Got it? You can think up the rest for yourself, or whatever."

Pedro finally seemed to come back to life, and nodded. He glanced up. "Yeah, right, thanks Bill. Owe you one, eh? Thanks Mick."

"You'll be right," the big old man said. "No worries, eh, none at all - part of the service."

He stood straight, stretching his back as he gazed about. "Better clear off now, don't you reckon? Never know who might be hanging around, some of those coons of yours maybe, or a few knob 'eads, like. Take it easy from here on, won't you mate?"

He glanced quickly down at Sky, adding, "You'll be a good lad too, won't you son. We won't be hearing much about you, will we, except maybe your new job and honest wages? Never too late to grow up, that's my opinion. Go and see Alf at the bakery when you're back on your feet, he might have something if you ask nice. Come over for a beer after you get settled and we'll teach you some real tricks."

Chapter Twenty Five

The phone was ringing in the front room out on the farm and Eric got up drowsily to answer it. He listened for a moment before hanging up, and went into the other room to wake Sunny.

"That was Brigit. They found your brother," he said softly. "He's dead. Looks like suicide, hose from the exhaust through the window."

"What? No, he wouldn't do that. Sky? No, don't believe it, He's too bloody cheeky."

"Not Sky, Daren. Sky's in hospital, had an accident apparently, came off his motorbike and cut his leg, or got caught by the explosion. Got a few cuts to his face as well, broken nose, black eye, and gravel rash. Pedro found him."

Sunny sat up in bed, shaking his head. "Daren wouldn't either. No, someone's got to him, Aedan I reckon. OD'ed him and made it look like suicide. That's what's happened."

"Yeah, might be. He pissed off suddenly and nobody can find him. Brian's not saying anything, says he doesn't know shit, he was with Brigit. Peters and Marchant copped it too, bomb under the cop car; blew up in the main street, shit everywhere. That's what the explosion was."

Sunny's eyes boggled and his jaw dropped. "Really? Fuck, eh? Fuckin' cunts. Fuck, yeah, shit, nobody'll be sorry those bastards got it. That's why Aiden's pissed off so quick, I bet. He done it, no worries, only one mad enough."

"Well, the other news is Brigit and Brian are going to Perth, taking Amelia. She wanted to know if you want to go with them, or stay here with Bill. You can stay with us if you want, and do home schooling with Karl."

By that time Daniel had been woken by their talking. He got up and stepped over to Sunny's bed and slipped in beside him. Sunny without thinking moved to make room for him, distracted by his own thoughts.

"Ah, well, I'll think about it. Better ask Bill first, see what he reckons. Tim and me are mates, I can live with them if I want, they won't mind. If I go with Brigit there'll just be a shit fight all the time, and I don't know anyone in Perth. Fuck, they're all cunts, serious. I'm just a kid."

He lay back in bed staring out the window, before noticing for the first time Daniel lying there at his side looking at him. Daniel leaned over and put his face into his, gazing into his eyes until he giggled and pushed him off. He sat up and got out of bed to wake Tim.

Eric returned to his room to rouse Lou, finding him already up and heading for the toilet, so he turned down to the kitchen to start breakfast.

When the boys came out Sunny went across to the TV and switched it on, expecting something on the morning news. He wasn't disappointed as the screen flashed with images of a demolished main block in town, and the local Member of Parliament inspecting the damage.

The Acting State Premier was on screen saying angrily, "This is not Belfast, or Beirut. We have no tolerance at all for this sort of activity." The Police Commissioner on a jump cut as if it were the same face said in reply, "It's not terrorism, you can't say that. It's an explosion resulting in the deaths of two people and injuring a young boy. If it's anything it's murder, and assault, and destruction of property."

The Major Crime Squad had been onsite since the previous evening, closing the street off while they went over it with a fine comb and removed what remained of the two policemen.

Fortunately there'd been only one other casualty, the reporter went on, a local teenager admitted to hospital with deep lacerations to his upper legs from flying glass, and minor facial injuries. He was under police guard as a potential witness to the crime.

Eric had started dishing out Weetbix all round when Chas drove up the track from the front gate in Wally's old truck and pulled up out front, with Nicolas in the front seat with Sarah, and all the others piled in the back.

When Nicolas came inside Sunny retreated to his room with Daniel and shut the door. The other two boys stood around awkwardly, embarrassed.

Nic turned straightaway on his heel and went back out, holding his hands up.

"Yeah, sorry," he said. "Come in, Sair. Everyone else go home, it's all right. No worries, sorry, we'll ride over later, along the back. The boys can ride their bikes if they want, OK?"

Eric watching them through the front window turned suddenly and went to his room, coming back with his guitar case. He went outside and handed it across to Chas, speaking quietly to him for a moment, then went back into the house. He glanced quickly at his brother on the way past, who nodded slightly and turned to follow. Sarah came up the steps and inside.

Chas put Eric's guitar gently on the front seat and gave the keys to Emma. He turned and went around to the back shed, staying out of the house. Alex went to jump out of the truck but Peter held him back, shaking his head. "We'll be right," he said, "no worries, boss."

Alex looked intently at him. "I'm not your boss. What's up with you? Been reading too many of those stupid bloody Phantom comics, or what?"

"Oh, yeah, Phantom comic, eh? Fuckin' purple underpants outside, tellin' Governor how to do it, savin' stupid black bastard, can't save himself yet, eh? We'll be right."

Chapter Twenty Six

Sam had his cameras set up on high platforms that Robbie knocked up for him, with a walkway between them so he could move back and forth above the audience without blocking their view of the stage, the timber decking laid with old carpet to deaden his footsteps.

Chas and Eric appeared on cue, in their clean and pressed western outfits and guitars. The crowd clapped in anticipation. The two on stage stood back, clapping themselves to welcome Karl in his hippie long hair and banjo as he came on and sat down, then Jennie with her violin.

Chas stepped up to the mike. "You all remember Jimmie Rodgers' *Muleskinner Blues*," he said, "and Bill Monroe's boys. This is our take on it. Hope you like it."

He turned to Eric and stepped back, flicking his thumb at the microphone. Eric hesitated, until Karl opened with his banjo and Chas followed straight away with his guitar, and Jennie looking at him took up the tune on her fiddle. Hooked right in, Eric stepped straight up to the mike and sang out in his breaking treble, working to hold his high notes.

Good morning captain
Good morning sky
Do you need another mule skinner
Out on your new line

Workin' on, the railroad
I'm rollin' all the time
I can pop my initials
On a mule any old time

I'm going to town
What do you want me to bring you back
Bring a walking cane
And a John B. Stetson hat

Hey little water boy

Bring that bucket 'round
If you don't like your job
Set your water bucket down . . . .

Taking a deep breath he let down his guitar and leaned into the microphone. Watching him, Chas leaned forward himself and waving his left hand during a chord break brought Karl and Jennie on.

The moment the piece finished Eric stood back and waved his right hand in turn to the others, then stepping across to Chas leaned over and whispered in his ear. Chas stood and shifting his chair back motioned Karl and Jennie forward. The moment they'd settled and without waiting for them Eric stepped up again to the microphone and sang,

Oh, I wish I had someone to love me, Someone to call me their own
Oh, I wish I had someone to live with, 'Cause I'm tired of living alone.
Oh, meet me tonight in the moonlight, Please meet me tonight all alone.
For I have a sad story to tell you, it's a story that's never been told . . . .

Up on top of the amphitheatre Alex sat back amazed. He leaned forward to listen, then sat back again shaking his head. An hour or so later, at the barbeque lunch, he made his way through the crowd to catch up with Nicolas and fingered him.

"Yeah, what, Nic?" he wanted to know.

"What what, Alex?"

"Why didn't you tell me about Eric? He's great!"

"You didn't ask, not that you'd listen."

Nicolas glanced at him, frowning. "I don't mean it's your fault Alex, that you don't listen like, you just can't, panoptic one-way glasses, conditioning, sort of. You can't read people, have to have every little thing explained. *Wadjela* are like that, until they break out; took me years to figure it out myself. Read Foucault, not about sex, *History of Sexuality* they're all into, I mean, *Birth of the Prison, Madness and Civilisation*; that stuff. Read J. D. Laing's *Bird of Paradise, The Divided Self.* That's where it's at, sort of. It's not people who are mad, it's the system."

Sarah was watching them from the end of the long trestle with their food where she stood with Sunny and the other two boys. Daniel was helping himself to a huge bowl of tropical fruit salad with lashings of ice-cream.

"Hey, Alex," Nicolas drew his attention back to what he was saying. "Um, I've been thinking about this, for the film, you know. Let Sair be the director, she'll be good; she knows me really well and knows what I want from the script. She can interpret it properly, the way I want. You be the producer. You're best at that, all right. We can show you the rest as we go along."

"Why don't you get Eric on national television? We can get him over to Tamworth," Alex went on, oblivious.

Nicolas stared at him, and shook his head. "He doesn't want to, that's why. Um, we've got to go look after Sunny, all right? I'll catch up with you later."

As he turned he bumped into Bill Hanna who'd just arrived with Mick Lewis.

"Ah, now, here's someone you really should meet, Alex, Sergeant First Class Emeritus Michael Patrick Lewis, not quite retired - that's just a rumour - we won't let him," he grinned.

The big man nodded, affectionately scruffing Nic's hair before taking Alex's hand for a warm solid shake. Peter appeared at his elbow from somewhere so he introduced him as well.

Nicolas ducked away to where Sarah was standing, leaving Alex and Peter with the old boys to get acquainted. After a quick parley they disappeared over the slope toward the swimming hole, Daniel noticed they'd gone and ran to catch up, taking his fruit salad with him.

Chapter Twenty Seven

To beat the traffic they left Monday afternoon, leaving Emma who wanted to work a while longer on some flute chords with her mother and Liz. She would come up to Perth with Marcus on Wednesday, in time for her Studio Fundamentals unit in Architecture with Robbie in the afternoon.

Nicolas stayed with Alex in Sam's flat, not that they had much time to work on the film since first assignments were due in two weeks, with four essays each to complete and hand in. Three ran to 1100 words, but the tricky one in English was only 500 words. But he'd settled into the place and moved a lot of his gear in, and anyway wanted to stay close to Alex for a while longer and get to know him better.

Things didn't turn out the way they expected. Halfway through the next week Bill Hanna rang to let them know Sunny was in hospital, on anti-depressant medication. He'd slipped into a black hole after they'd returned to Perth, not getting along so well with Tim's parents and Pedro calling in only once with money for his keep. Sky was out of hospital and hobbling about on crutches. He'd taken over Brigit's big caravan at the back of the house she was renting, refusing to budge while the owner simply cut his losses and got new tenants for the house.

Nicolas nodded thoughtfully. He turned to Sam and asked if it was OK for Sunny to come up and stay a while, explaining what had happened, but Sam simply shrugged, used to teenagers in and out of the place so one more would make little difference, and went back to cleaning his smaller still camera.

He then said to Alex, "Well, I've got a job for you, Alex. I need you to bond with Sunny when he gets here. He likes you and he's seriously close to Sair, so I think that's the best thing."

Alex glanced up from his essay and nodded.

He put the phone back to his ear and asked Bill if he could sort it with Pedro to get him out of hospital and maybe have him stay at his place for a few days, at least until they could get him up to Perth. Bill said he'd arrange it, suggesting he might bring him up himself and come back the same day, bringing Daniel along for the ride. He'd never been to Perth.

Sam interrupted saying Sunny has to go to school, what were they going to do about that? Who was going to drop him off and pick him up all the time, and make sure he does his homework?

Alex looked up sharply. "We will," he said. "We'll take turns. I don't want to argue about it."

Nicolas asked Bill to hang on a minute.

Sam went to say something else but Alex quickly pointed out that's precisely what he'd done for him when he was twelve, and brought Peter down from the desert at the same age. Where would they have been otherwise? What's the problem now? What's different?

Sam put the camera down. "Well, for one thing," he said, exasperated, "I'm the only legal bloody adult around the place. Back then there were only the two of you, and how many are there now? Ten? You're joking."

"Well, don't be like that," Alex challenged him. "Eight, isn't it? Julian only came over the once, and I don't think he'll be back. With Sunny it'll be nine, but there's Marcus, and Bill, and Jennie and Liz, and Chas, and I had a good yarn with Mick Lewis about the kids; he's right I agree with him. And we're at Uni, and Sunny'll be in school. There's our lecturers, and his new teachers, be a lot better for him. Don't be such a prick."

Nicolas followed the exchange, gazing steadily at Alex, watching his face. He glanced at Sam who picked up his camera again shaking his head.

"I want this to be unanimous," he said. "We all need to agree."

Alex flashed impatiently at him. "Of course we agree, dumb arse. What sort of people do you think we are? We're only talking detail, right?"

"Anyway," he added, "Sunny's a real nice kid. I like him a lot. He doesn't deserve to be treated so badly as that . . . . ."

He stood suddenly and threw his pen angrily down, going across to the kitchen pretending to get something from the fridge, somewhere out of sight. "Just shut the fuck up, right? Just do it."

Nicolas smiled to himself and speaking briefly to Bill put the phone down. He went into their room and started packing his gear, then coming back out picked up the phone again and rang Sarah.

Chapter Twenty Eight

Two days later Alex arrived home from his late lecture to find Bill with Sunny on the doorstep, and Daniel still in the Landcruiser scared to get out. Nicolas had cleared out, and Sam was away somewhere filming. He let them in.

Bill brought in Sunny's bags and left them on the living room floor. With a quick glance at Alex he went straight back out. Daniel by this time was hiding on the floor behind the front seat. He opened the back passenger door and bending down picked him up, carried him inside and set him down, holding him close so he wouldn't bolt.

The little boy was shaking, eyes wide, gazing up at all the desks and computers and cameras, and bookshelves and gear. He hid behind Bill, who instinctively put his hand around and ruffled his long hair.

"You be right, mate?" Bill asked Sunny. "Better get back, eh, before dark."

Sunny nodded and stepped forward to shake his hand, not saying anything.

Bill turned to Alex, telling him to get Sunny off the medication straight away, the sooner the better. Antidepressants took a month to kick in, and he'd only been on them a week so no harm would come of it. That wasn't the problem.

"Yeah, Bill," Alex leaned back against his desk. "No worries, it's all right. You look after Daniel, is that OK?"

He stepped forward and reaching around took Daniel's hand. The wild tangle-haired boy looked up at him and after a moment came around and jumped into his arms; face right into his own face. He held him a moment smiling at him before passing him back to Bill, and ushered them outside.

Alone with Sunny he picked up his backpack and his couple of bags and carried them into their room. He threw them on the other bed and sat down on his own. Sam still hadn't changed things around as he'd threatened when Sarah said she wanted to spend more time there, so there was plenty of space.

Sunny came in tentatively and sat on the bed, leaning back possessively against his belongings. He reached down and adjusted his crotch, looking intently at Alex.

"Yeah, well, I'm not gay, is that all right?" he said. "With you I mean, Alex."

"What? What the fuck? You're worried about that? That's your problem?"

Alex sat back, confused.

"Are you a gay boy, Sunny? Worried I might tell, if you live with us? Is that it? Why would I worry, we've been swimming, I know what you look like, I mean, we're all the same. You're twelve now, like I was, same age then, and you're getting pubes; what do you expect? Everyone does, it's just what happens. What are you talking about?"

Sunny stared at him, eyes wide, then frowned and blinked, and looked down. He looked up intently again.

"Yeah but," he said quietly, "I was with my mates, and you were with your friends, and you're hell famous and I'm just a kid. Don't fuck me, Alex, all right? I don't want people fucking me, like, that's it, anyone."

"Is that why you were in hospital, on medication?"

"No."

"Why then? Why put it on me?"

"I didn't, did I? I only wanted to know. Nobody ever told me this stuff."

He stood and undressed, daring Alex to make anything of it - the two of them alone together - and taking a clean towel from his pack went for a shower.

Alex sat back, thinking about what Nicolas had said about *Wadjela*, and his coming of age with Peter, and Sam, and the old fellas up in the desert, and finally got up to follow suit.

In the cramped shower recess he hung his towel on the rail waiting for Sunny to finish.

"Nic said I've got to bond with you, Sunny, you all right with that?"

Sunny pulled the plastic curtain back and stepped out. "Yeah, well, Nic's good but sometimes he's a bit if a wanker; knows too much, thinks he does. What do you reckon?"

Alex frowned, looking away. "I don't know," he said, stepping into the cubicle. He turned the water back on, leaving the curtain open. "Nic's hell deep, fucked if I know, really, like as if he's been to heaven and hell and back and survived, and I thought I'd only been to hell. You think you know him, and then you don't, like he's a stranger again and you have to start all over with him. He was onto me straight away, like, knew everything."

Sunny stood up straight from drying his legs and backside.

"He got fucked up the arse, and their Mum topped herself," he said suddenly. "You didn't know that, did you?"

"Simon, his younger brother, eh, Eric's twin brother, was killed and their Dad Jack slashed his arms and died of it, like, bled to death, in the back alley. Dinky and his stupid mates did it, Dinky Kulinsky, but after Nic tried to hang himself Mick Lewis found out and arrested them; had them convicted. Dinky got twelve years. That started the shit in town, well, not really, 'cause Dinky's Mum was the social worker sort of, self-appointed, and when she went down there was nobody for us, 'til Bill got back from Asia. But she was a bitch. She ran the school P&C and bossed the whole town. Everyone hated her."

Alex stood under the pouring water, listening intently, and during the pause bent down to wash his legs and feet. Sunny finished drying himself and combed his hair in the mirror. He went out and came back again in pyjama bottoms with a new toothbrush and leaned over the sink to brush his teeth.

When he was done he straightened up and turned to Alex still there in the shower. "Something you should know about Eric too. He hated Nic, when he was little, reckoned he was in strife all the time because of him. Nic was always in trouble at school, none of the teachers could handle him. That's why they started the home school out on Wally's place, he's the reason. But their mother was a real hard case anyway, serious man-hater; it's just that Nicolas copped the blame for it, for everything. Grant used to beat him up too."

"See, um, after Grant went up to Wallaga Simon was living with Nic on the farm but Eric was living on the street, trying to be a bigshot with the Kulinsky boys. He's the one who set Jack up, his own father, because he was gay. The boys were giving him a working over when Nic and Simon arrived. They didn't expect it, that's how it happened. After old Wally got killed by the lightning Nic forgave him, and got Mick to pick him up and bring him out to the farm. Then they got him cleaned up, him and Robbie, and Emma found him a nice girlfriend but she got killed last year in a car accident. Chas gave him a job with the cattle, and taught him guitar."

He shook his head, frowning slightly, as if to shake out a bad memory. "Gee they're good people, the Larkins, bloody amazing" he said after a moment. "People in town are real cunts. They don't give a fuck about anybody. It's just a bad town, serious. I don't know where any of us kids'd be without Nic, strange as he is, or Bill or Mick Lewis."

Alex stepped out of the shower and shoved Sunny's shoulder a little, pushing him half out the door to make room to dry himself.

"Is that why you're here? Because you trust Nic, is that right?"

"Yeah, sort of. Brigit's gonna freak when she finds out I'm here, but it'll be right. Bill's gonna help me with it, and Pedro's already agreed. She only wants me to look after Amelia so she and Brian can go partying. Here I can go to school, and you help me with my homework. That'd be good, yeah, real good. When I leave school Chas might give me a job with the cattle, and I can stay on the farm, that'd be hell wicked. I hope he does."

When Sam arrived home two hours later he found them in bed with the light on, still talking.

Alex had a nine o'clock lecture next day so Sam had the job of taking Sunny to start his new school. He decided on Churchlands Senior High School for its proximity and reputation, and arrived there with Sunny in tow and their paperwork in order.

After school Nicolas came over and gave Sam the wad of money for Sunny that Pedro had given him at Easter, and hadn't spent. While he was there Sarah arrived from her Archaeology lecture and went in to check on Sunny, to see how he was. Alex was going over his new reading list with him, and came out to get some cash he could take to school next day. He needed a new uniform as well, just shirts and a pullover since his old trousers were the same colour.

The four of them then decided to go back to Marcus' place and leave Sam in peace.

Chapter Twenty Nine

Peter called in mid-morning on Thursday to catch Alex for their Anthropology lecture, and they went back over to Marcus' place to get Sarah and Nic. They'd changed their schedule around after Sunny arrived, so instead of the late afternoon lecture they caught the one at eleven so Alex would be back by time Sunny arrived home from school. They didn't all need to change but they did anyway because of their different tutorial times, which they could do nothing about because the course coordinator had strict rules.

Nicolas came out with some interesting news.

"Sunny's Mum's been arrested," he said quietly, "her and Brian. Cops found Aedan's car and stripped it, found blood in the boot. They knew Brian had been driving it and got suspicious when he and Brigit left town so quick, so they hammered him until he showed them where the body was."

"What? Brian murder him?"

"No, shit no, he only buried him they reckon. The autopsy showed he was killed by a piece of shrapnel from the car blast - the one that killed Peters and Marchant - same as Sky's legs, but went right through him, through his heart. They fucked up, mistimed the thing. Aedan and Sky were still too close apparently. When they picked up Sky he spilled the beans. They offered him indemnity if he told them everything so he said he helped set it up because the cops were ripping off his drug money, that he owed Aedan. He had too, or Aedan was going to kill him."

"So, ah, accessory to murder, apparently, both of them, and something else about acts of terror, all that stuff. Brigit's in jail too, on remand awaiting trial. I reckon the DPP will push it through quick, get it done fast so the government can go to the next election on it."

"What about Daren? What are they doing about that?"

"Nothing. Suicide. Drug psychosis they said, completely separate."

Alex turned sideways and took Nic's arm, and they stopped. "We'll need to rewrite our script. All this needs to go in," he said.

Nicolas looked at him, blinking. "Yes, that's right, why not? That's what it needs, yes, I agree, let's do it."

Sarah stepped in. "Nobody will believe it; we'll have to fictionalize the whole thing, or it just won't come across. Why don't we write a new script, or revise the old one, I mean, rewrite it?"

"Yes, suspension of disbelief, that's it," Nicolas replied. "What do you think is the problem we need to address, in this context anyway?"

Sarah glanced quickly at him, then turned to Alex.

"Um, well," she began, "Alex, you do need to know, really, how Nic sees the world; we have to keep reminding him the way it is. It's like, until he was 13 he thought he'd landed on the wrong planet, and after that he thought it was the right planet but it'd been invaded by all these plaster statue people, and machine people, and, like, trolls, that are demented, and remnant humans had to protect themselves from them somehow. They're still not human, I agree, they're real bad arse shits and good riddance. They hurt people really bad, especially the boys. The girls don't get it much better, but anyway, that's how all this came about."

"He's right, in a lot of ways, and we all agree," she went on. "It's just a weird way to think, and it doesn't communicate very well, especially those boys so we don't say anything to them directly we only let them have their space, and attach themselves to where they want, and follow their nose, and it just works, it's good."

Alex looked at her curiously. "You don't let them attach, Sair, you bring them on."

"That's just you, Alex, 'cause you're such a drop dead spunk."

She paused. "But they like you different from the way they like me; you and Nic, and Bill you know, that's what I'm talking about. They look up to you, it's not the same, and anyway, they don't get enough mothering."

"Why don't we focus on where the money might be stashed," Nic interrupted, "and leave our private business out of it. Sky must have owed him $70-80,000 for Aedan Donovan to carry on the way he did, like, crazy, and it must be somewhere. We can make it a documentary, yes, that's it, a treasure hunt, and work the rest of the detail in around it."

"Don't give them too much detail, too many clues," Alex added after a moment. "If we find it ourselves we just won't say anything. You must have an idea where it might be, Nic; you grew up here and know the place inside out."

Nic flashed a quick glance at him, a slight smile on his face, but didn't reply. The three walked on a little not saying anything, then looked at one another nodding agreement.

Peter stood watching them with a peculiar look, shaking his head.

THE END

ABOUT THE AUTHOR

Born in England in 1951, Tom Fisher migrated to Australia during the 1970s as an aspiring young teacher. Initially attracted by the legendary toughness and independence of the Australian bushman he soon started to notice perplexing anomalies. Eventually retiring from teaching he returned to university to complete a specialist degree in literature, and is now a full time writer.